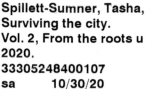

Surviving the City Vol. 2

From the Roots Up

Tasha Spillett

Natasha Donovan

HIGHWATER
PRESS

Canada Council   Conseil des Arts
for the Arts   du Canada

We acknowledge the support of the Canada Council for the Arts.
Nous remercions le Conseil des arts du Canada de son soutien.

HighWater Press gratefully acknowledges the financial support of the Province of Manitoba through the Department of Sport, Culture and Heritage and the Manitoba Book Publishing Tax Credit, and the Government of Canada through the Canada Book Fund (CBF), for our publishing activities.

Thank you to the following people who helped with the creation of this book:
Elder Albert McLeod, Cree translations and Two-Spirit review
Carissa Copenace, Anishinaabemowin translations

HighWater Press is an imprint of Portage & Main Press.
Printed and bound in Canada by Friesens
Design by Relish New Brand Experience
Cover art by Natasha Donovan
Lettering by Donovan Yaciuk

Library and Archives Canada Cataloguing in Publication

Title: Surviving the city. Vol. 2, From the roots up / Tasha Spillett ; [illustrated by] Natasha Donovan

Names: Spillett-Sumner, Tasha, 1988- author. | Donovan, Natasha, illustrator.

Identifiers: Canadiana (print) 2020015737X | Canadiana (ebook) 20200157434 | ISBN 9781553798989 (softcover) | ISBN 9781553798996 (EPUB) | ISBN 9781553799009 (PDF)

Subjects: LCGFT: Graphic novels.

Classification: LCC PN6733.S65 S87 2020 | DDC j741.5/971—dc23

23 22 21 20   1 2 3 4 5

HIGHWATER PRESS   THE DEBWE SERIES

www.highwaterpress.com
Winnipeg, Manitoba
Treaty 1 Territory and homeland of the Métis Nation

For the ones resting below and those rising above.
–TS

For Haley, who has been a source of courage
for two decades and counting.

–ND

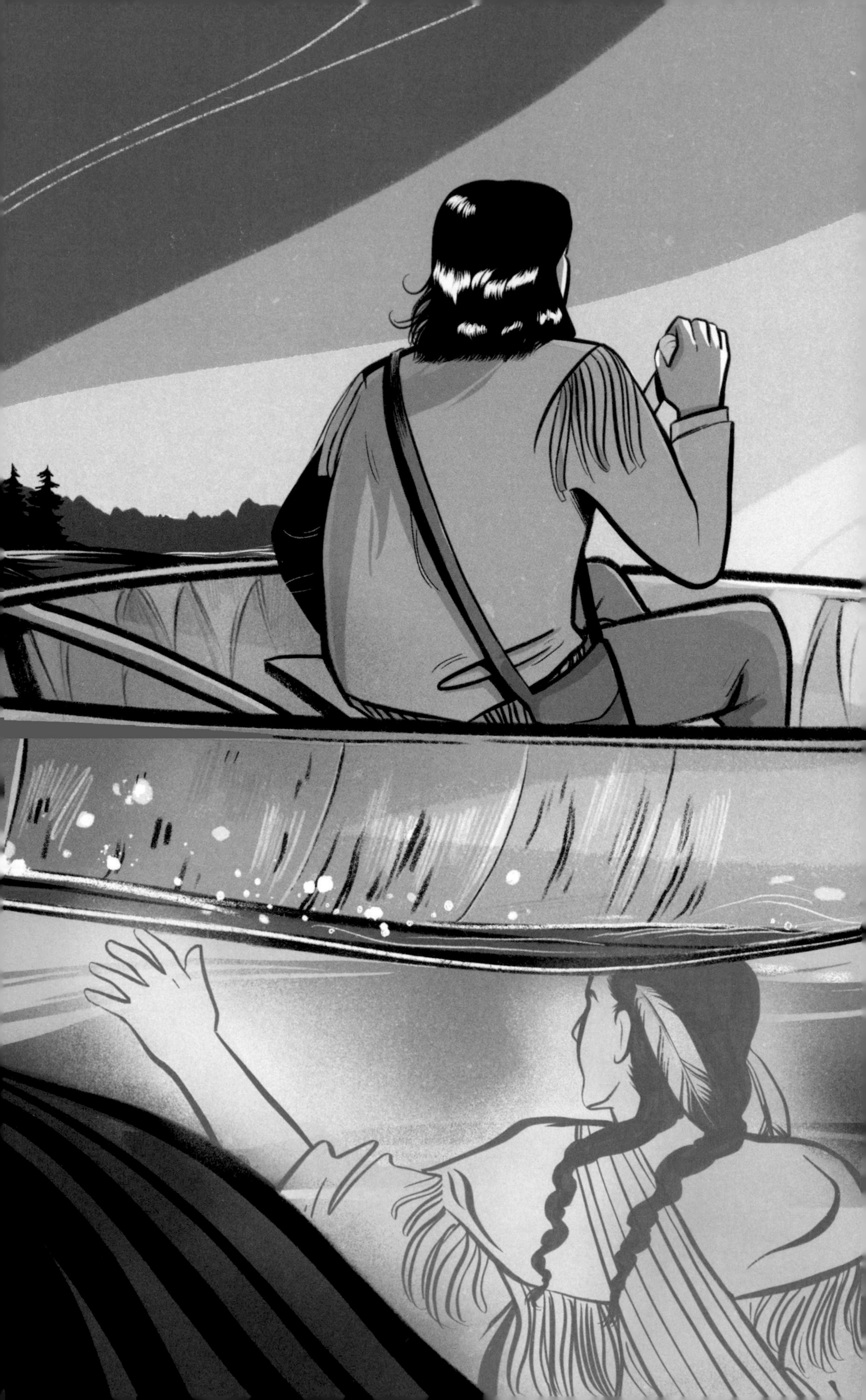

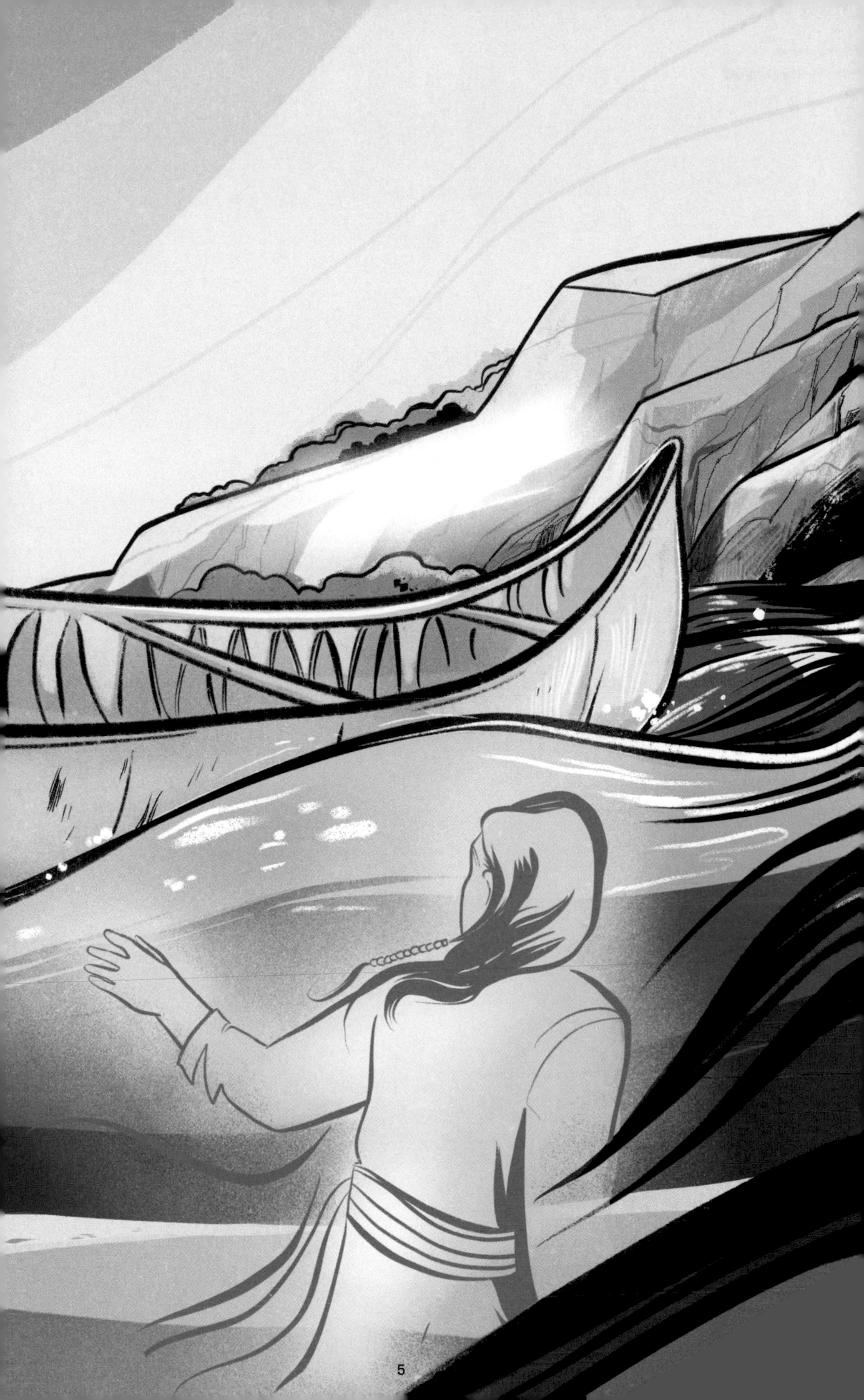

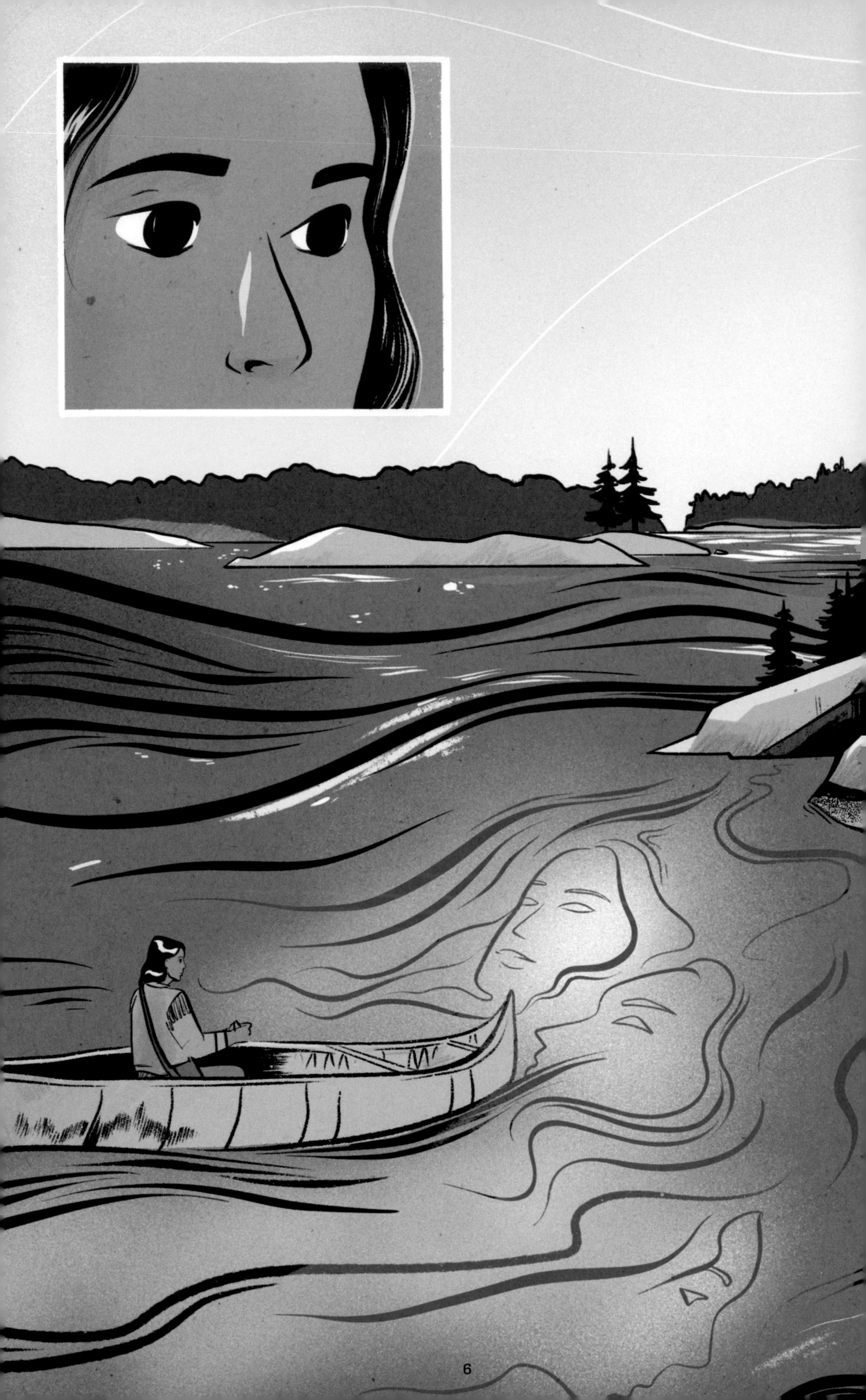

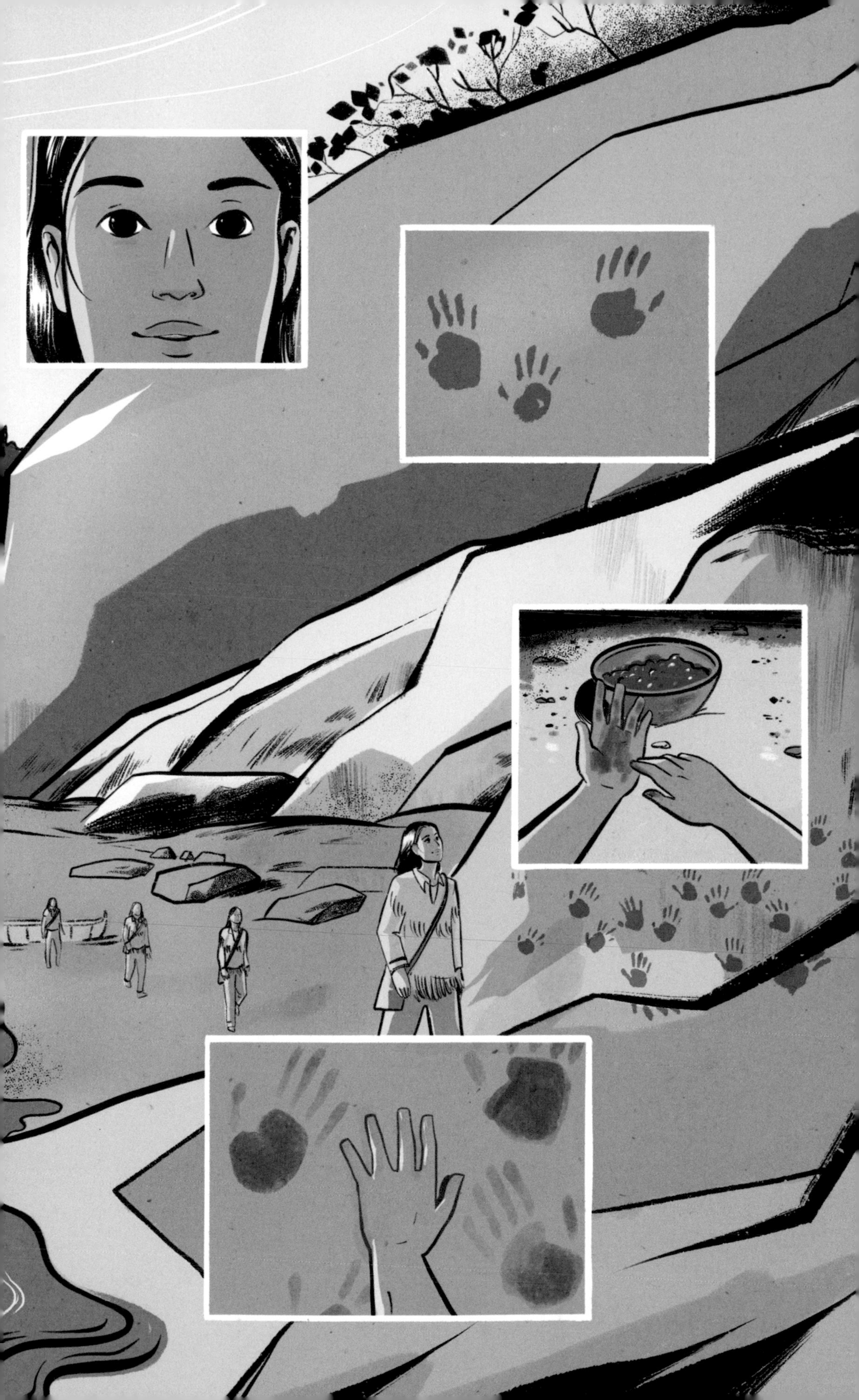

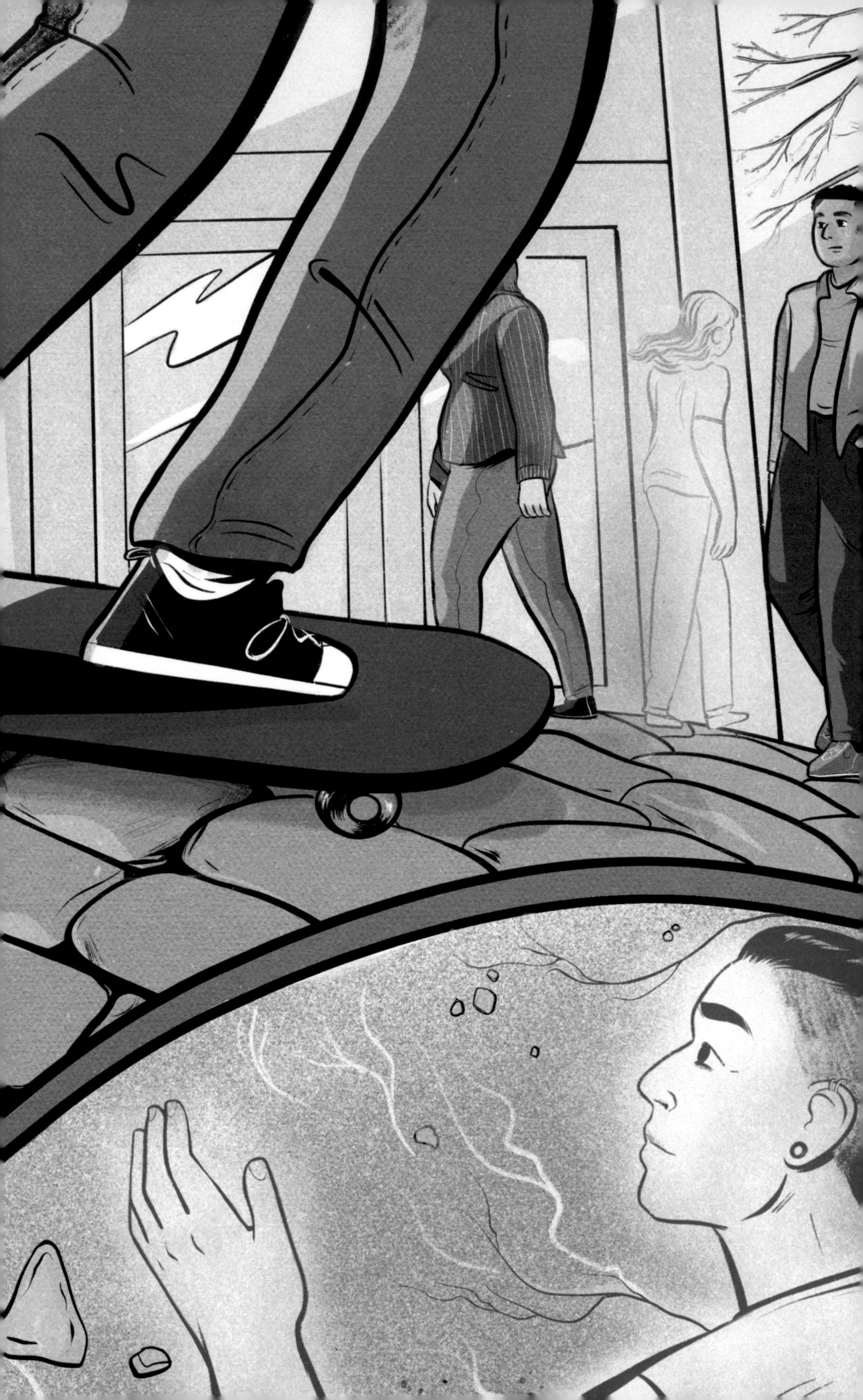

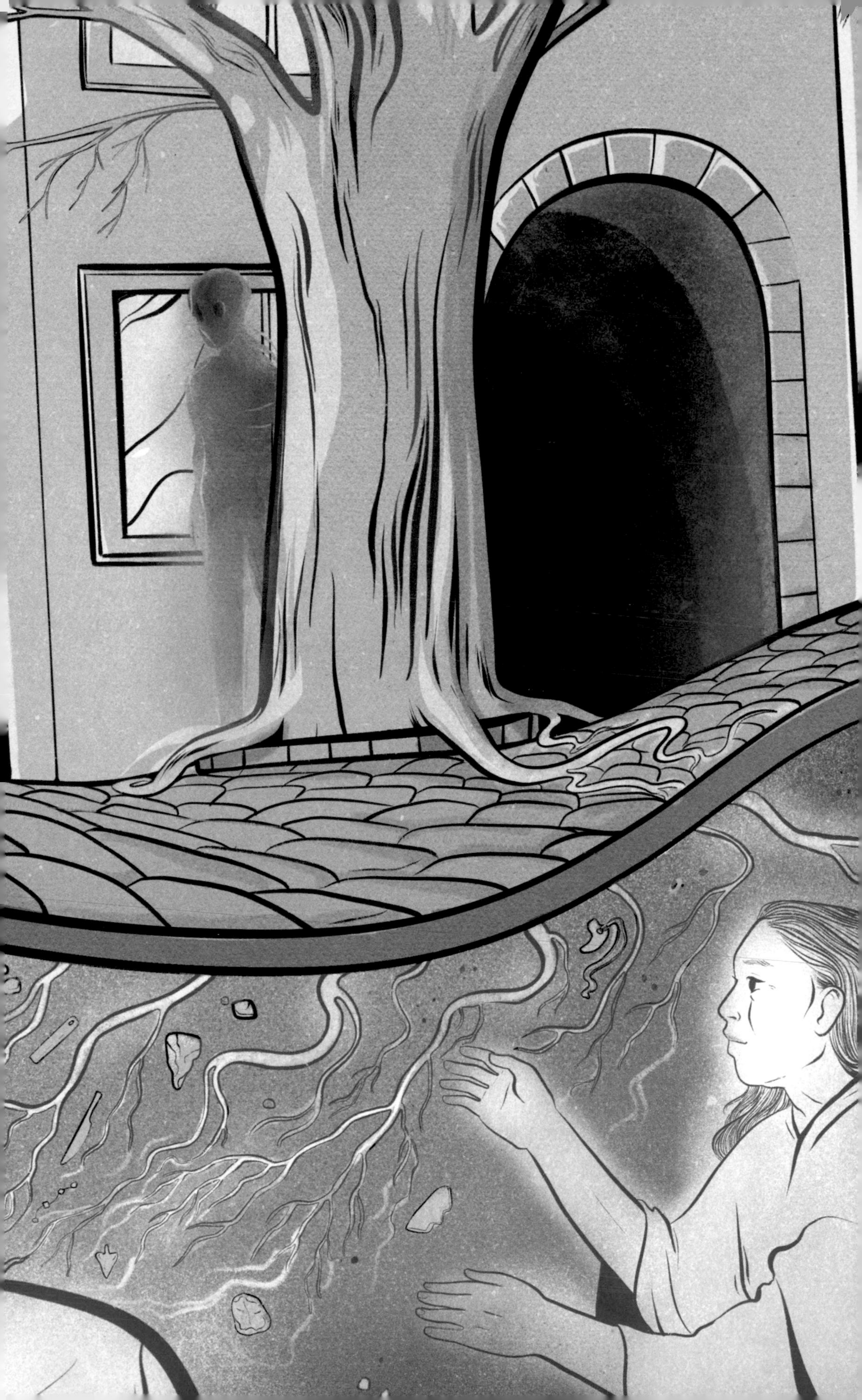

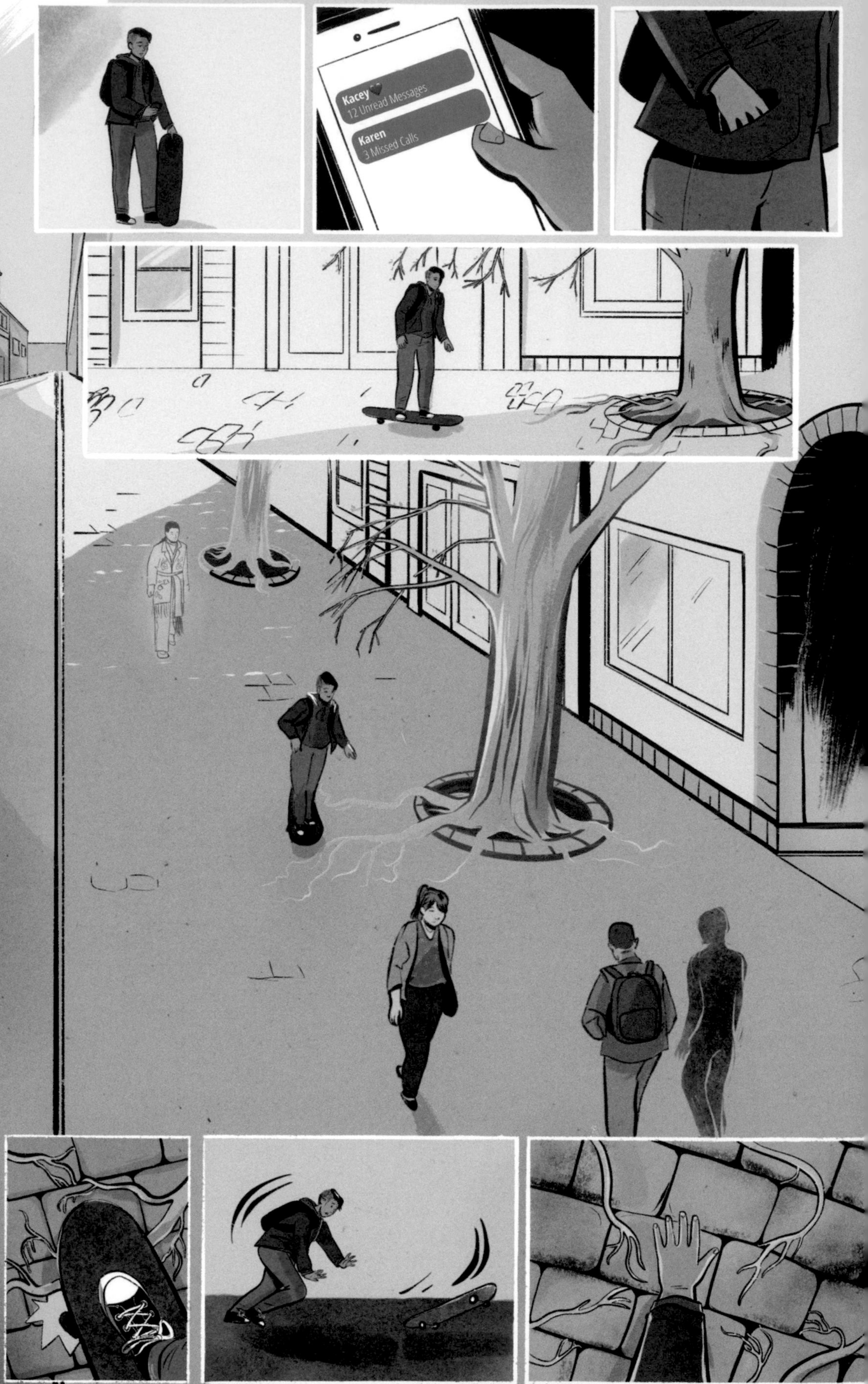
Kacey
12 Unread Messages
Karen
3 Missed Calls

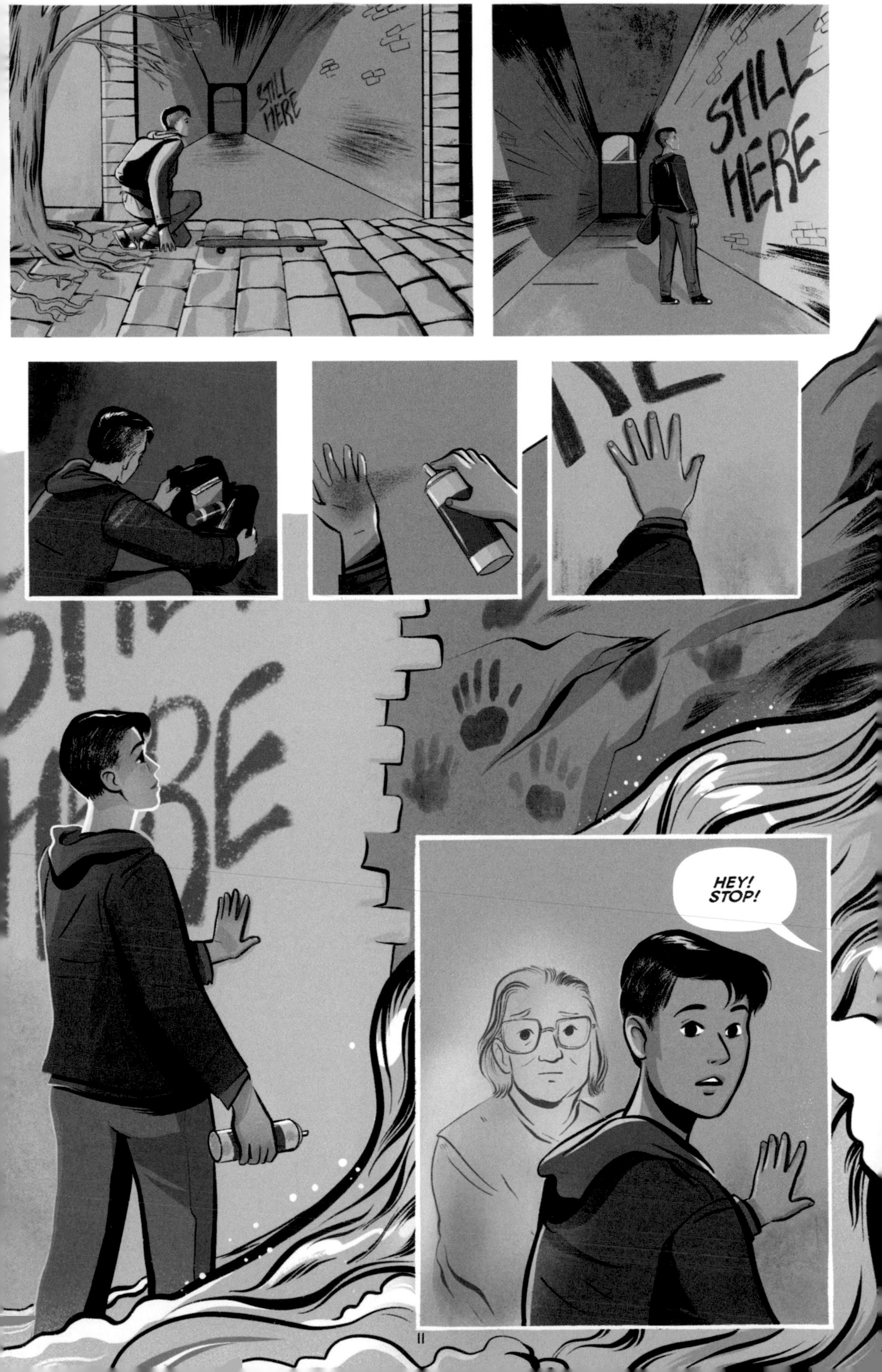
STILL HERE
STILL HERE
HEY! STOP!

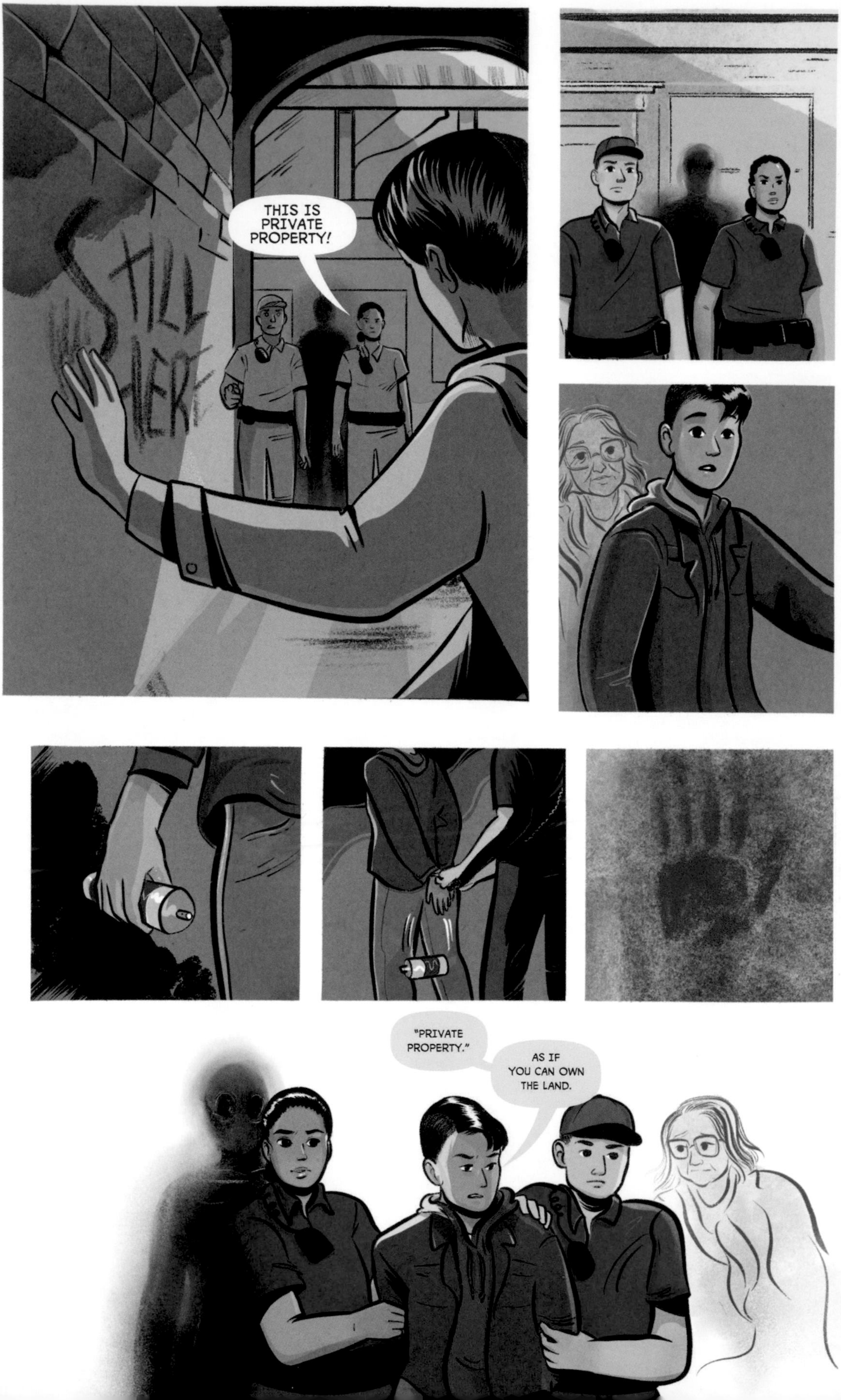
STILL
HERE
THIS IS PRIVATE PROPERTY!
"PRIVATE PROPERTY."
AS IF YOU CAN OWN THE LAND.

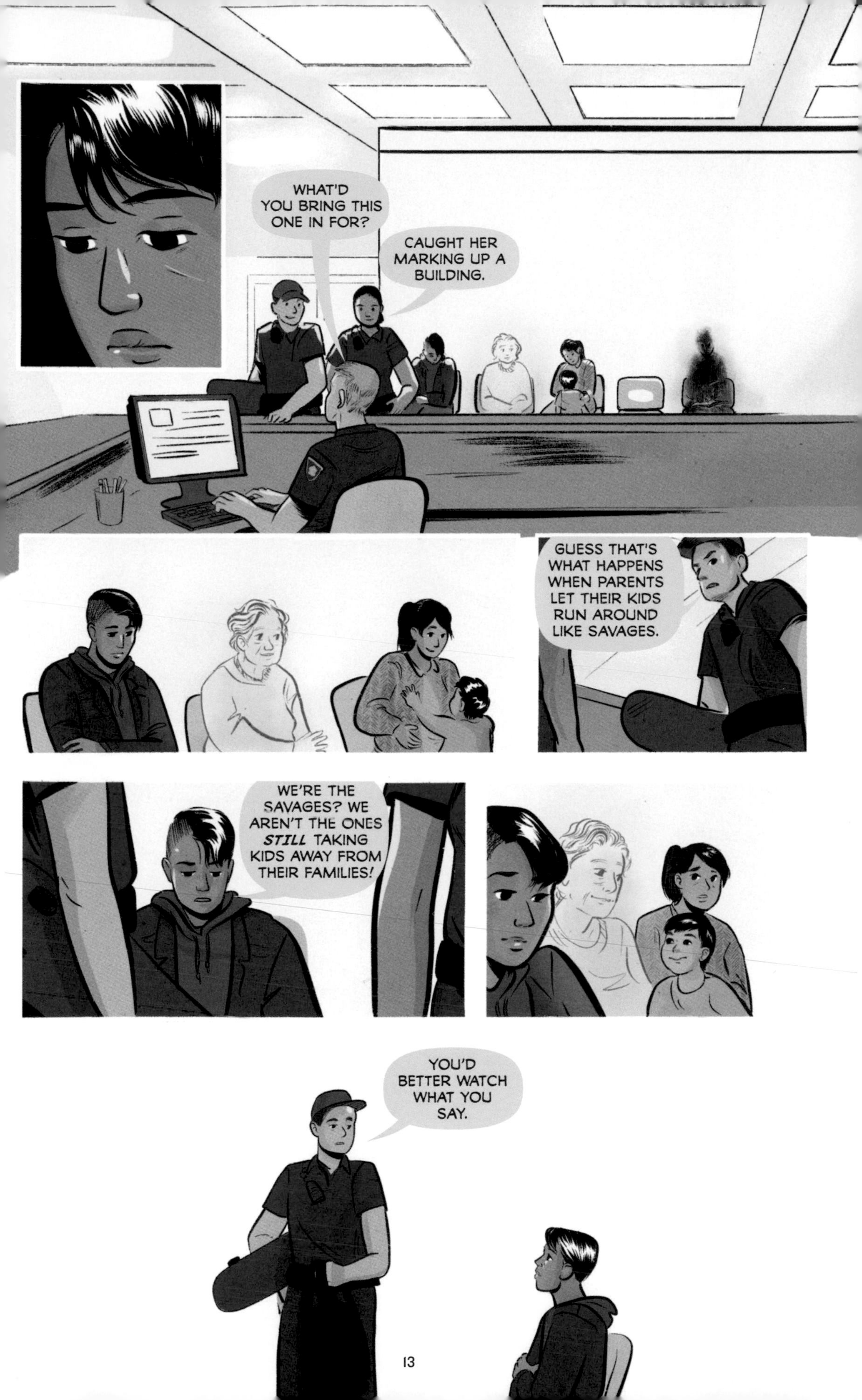
WHAT'D YOU BRING THIS ONE IN FOR?
CAUGHT HER MARKING UP A BUILDING.
GUESS THAT'S WHAT HAPPENS WHEN PARENTS LET THEIR KIDS RUN AROUND LIKE SAVAGES.
WE'RE THE SAVAGES? WE AREN'T THE ONES *STILL* TAKING KIDS AWAY FROM THEIR FAMILIES!
YOU'D BETTER WATCH WHAT YOU SAY.

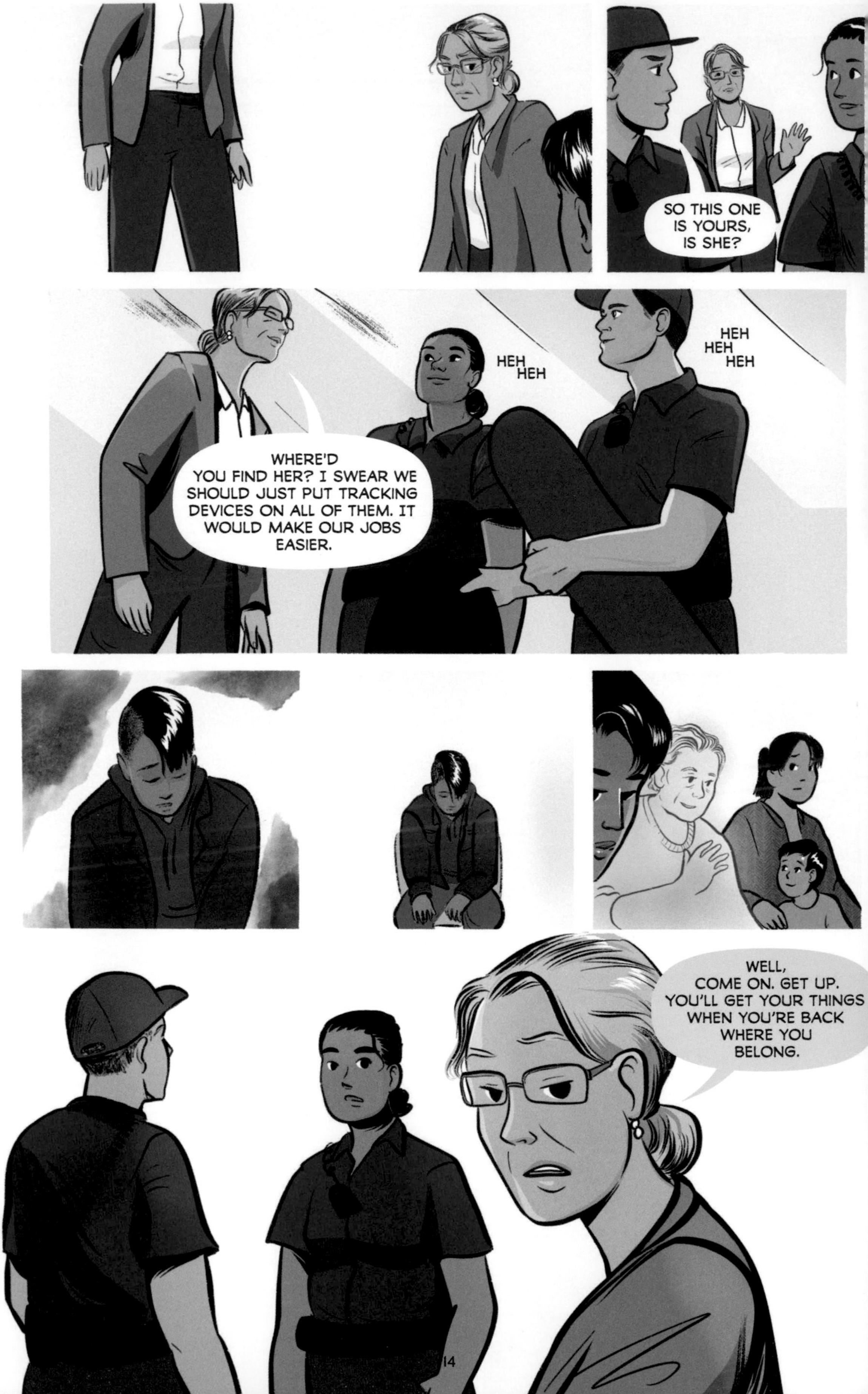
SO THIS ONE IS YOURS, IS SHE?
HEH HEH
HEH HEH HEH
WHERE'D YOU FIND HER? I SWEAR WE SHOULD JUST PUT TRACKING DEVICES ON ALL OF THEM. IT WOULD MAKE OUR JOBS EASIER.
WELL, COME ON. GET UP. YOU'LL GET YOUR THINGS WHEN YOU'RE BACK WHERE YOU BELONG.

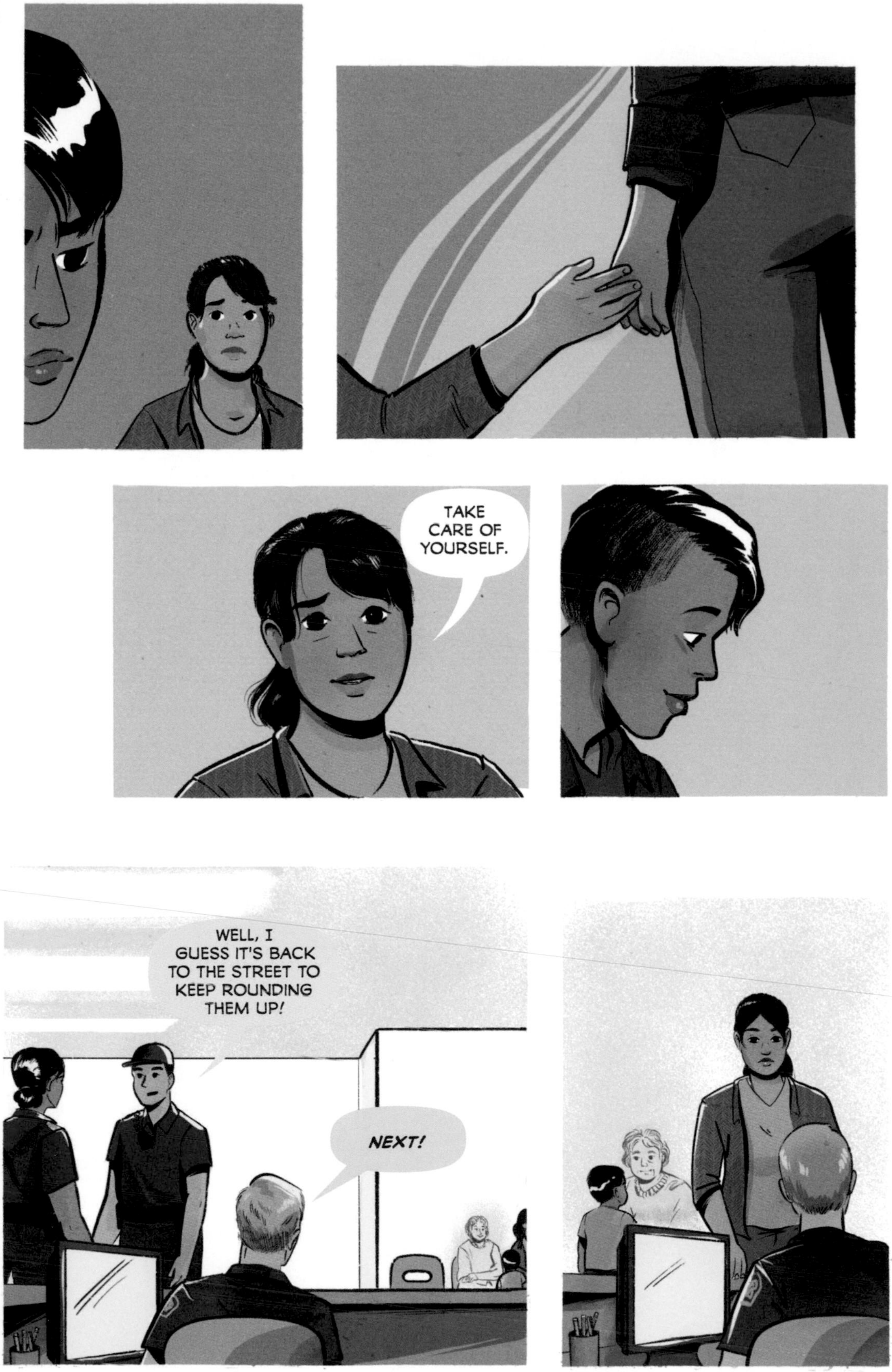
TAKE CARE OF YOURSELF.
WELL, I GUESS IT'S BACK TO THE STREET TO KEEP ROUNDING THEM UP!
NEXT!

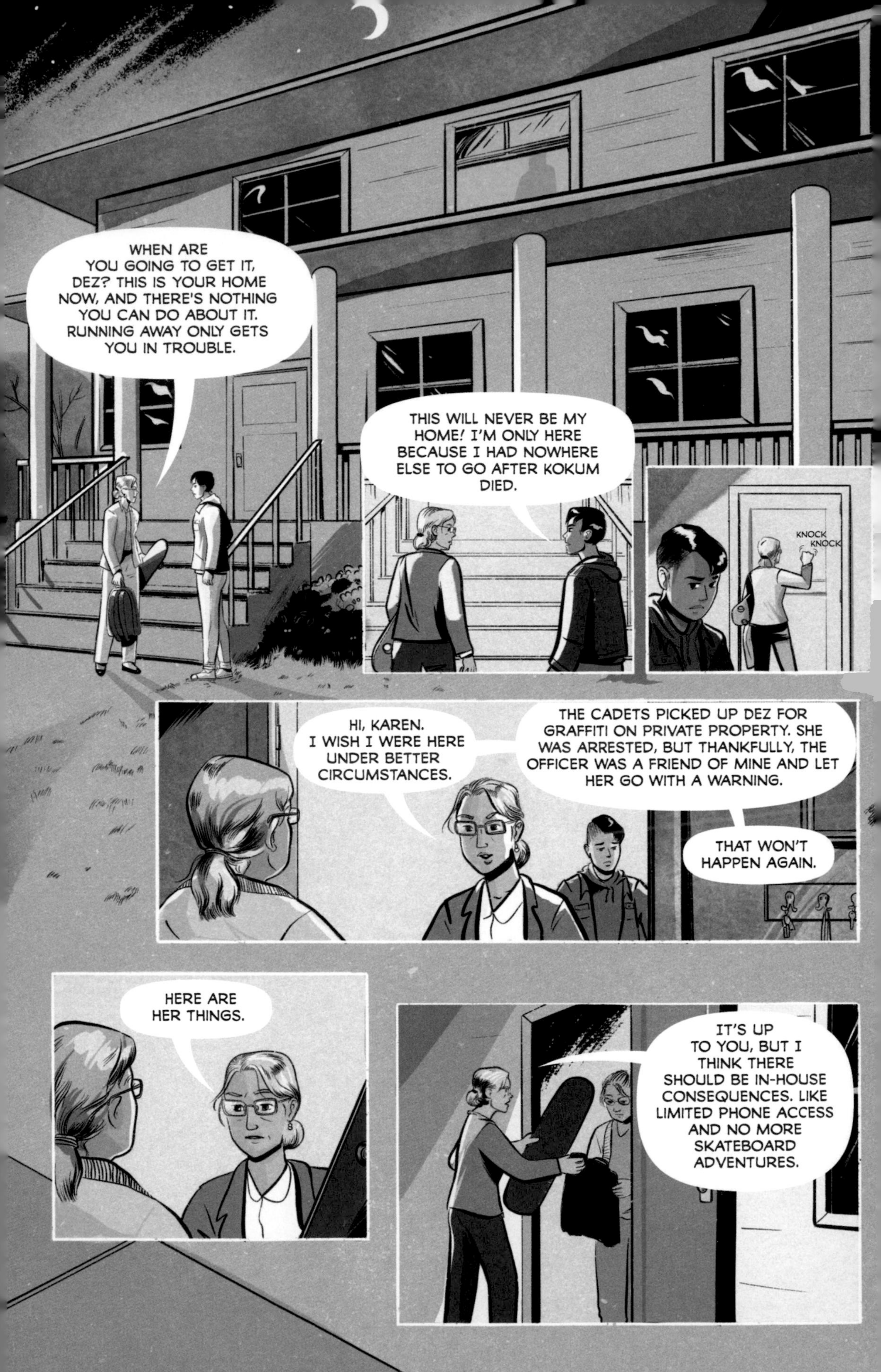
WHEN ARE YOU GOING TO GET IT, DEZ? THIS IS YOUR HOME NOW, AND THERE'S NOTHING YOU CAN DO ABOUT IT. RUNNING AWAY ONLY GETS YOU IN TROUBLE.
THIS WILL NEVER BE MY HOME! I'M ONLY HERE BECAUSE I HAD NOWHERE ELSE TO GO AFTER KOKUM DIED.
KNOCK KNOCK
HI, KAREN. I WISH I WERE HERE UNDER BETTER CIRCUMSTANCES.
THE CADETS PICKED UP DEZ FOR GRAFFITI ON PRIVATE PROPERTY. SHE WAS ARRESTED, BUT THANKFULLY, THE OFFICER WAS A FRIEND OF MINE AND LET HER GO WITH A WARNING.
THAT WON'T HAPPEN AGAIN.
HERE ARE HER THINGS.
IT'S UP TO YOU, BUT I THINK THERE SHOULD BE IN-HOUSE CONSEQUENCES. LIKE LIMITED PHONE ACCESS AND NO MORE SKATEBOARD ADVENTURES.

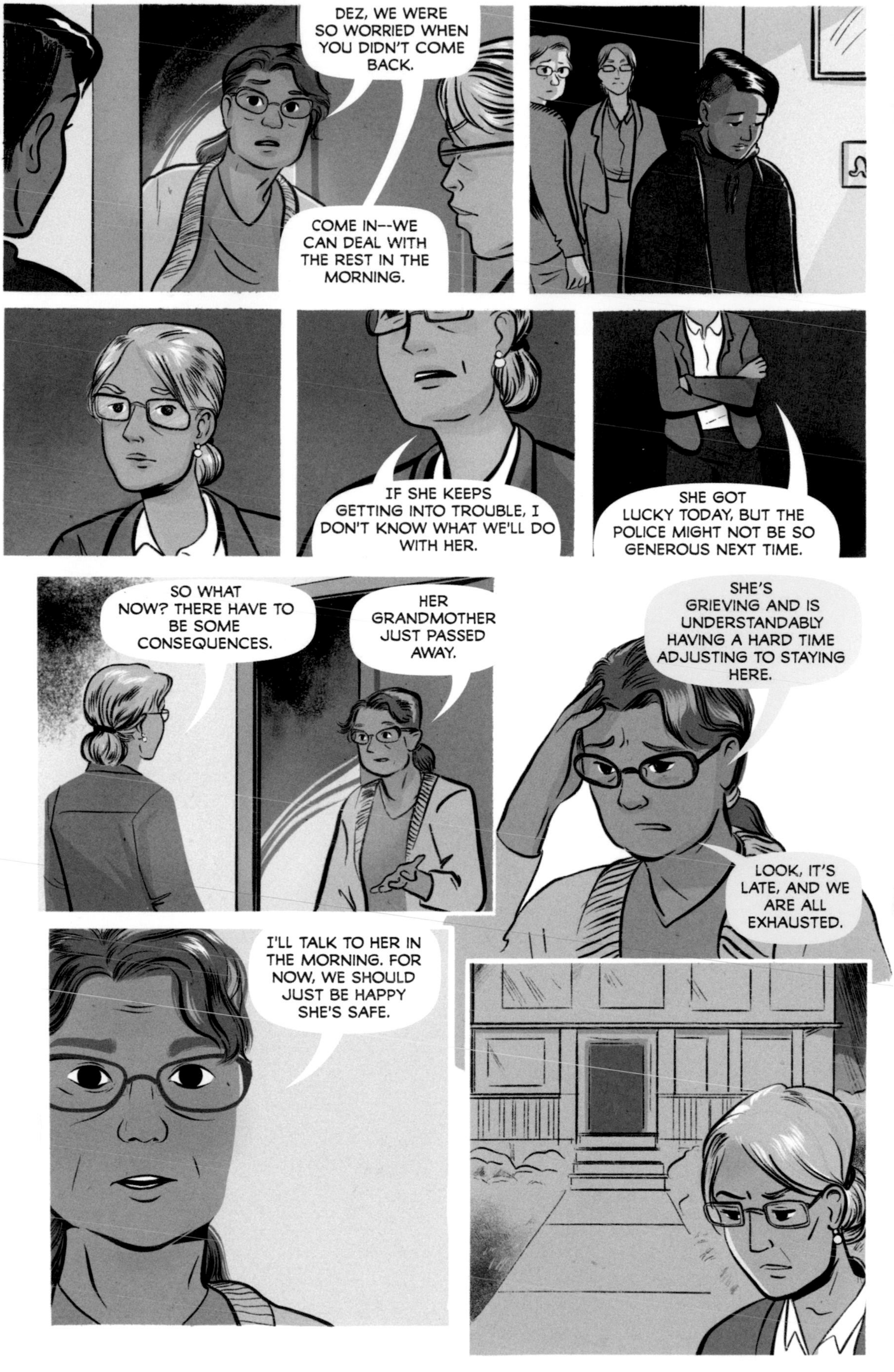
DEZ, WE WERE SO WORRIED WHEN YOU DIDN'T COME BACK.
COME IN--WE CAN DEAL WITH THE REST IN THE MORNING.
IF SHE KEEPS GETTING INTO TROUBLE, I DON'T KNOW WHAT WE'LL DO WITH HER.
SHE GOT LUCKY TODAY, BUT THE POLICE MIGHT NOT BE SO GENEROUS NEXT TIME.
SO WHAT NOW? THERE HAVE TO BE SOME CONSEQUENCES.
HER GRANDMOTHER JUST PASSED AWAY.
SHE'S GRIEVING AND IS UNDERSTANDABLY HAVING A HARD TIME ADJUSTING TO STAYING HERE.
LOOK, IT'S LATE, AND WE ARE ALL EXHAUSTED.
I'LL TALK TO HER IN THE MORNING. FOR NOW, WE SHOULD JUST BE HAPPY SHE'S SAFE.

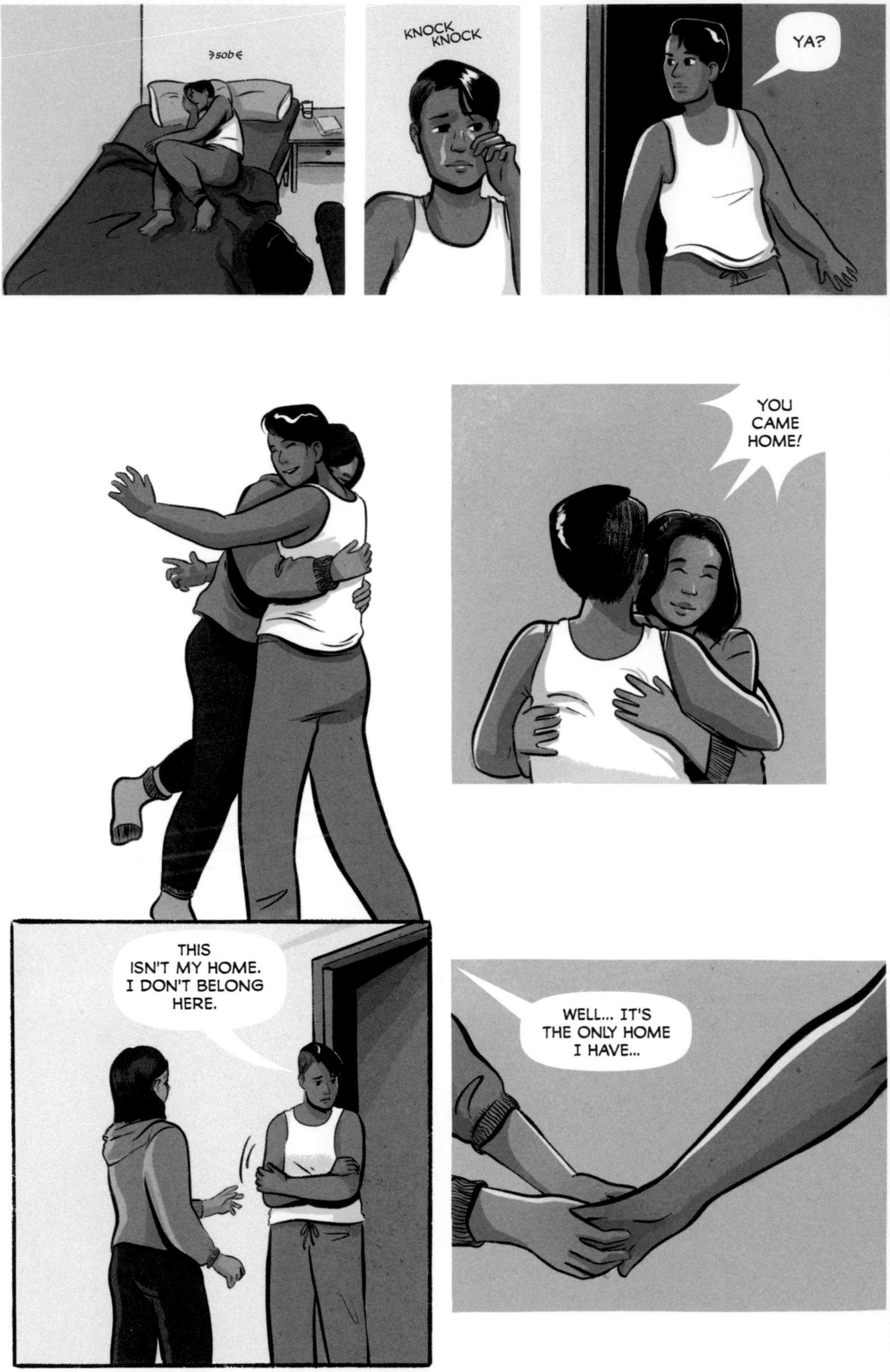

⋺sob⋲
KNOCK KNOCK
YA?
YOU CAME HOME!
THIS ISN'T MY HOME. I DON'T BELONG HERE.
WELL... IT'S THE ONLY HOME I HAVE...

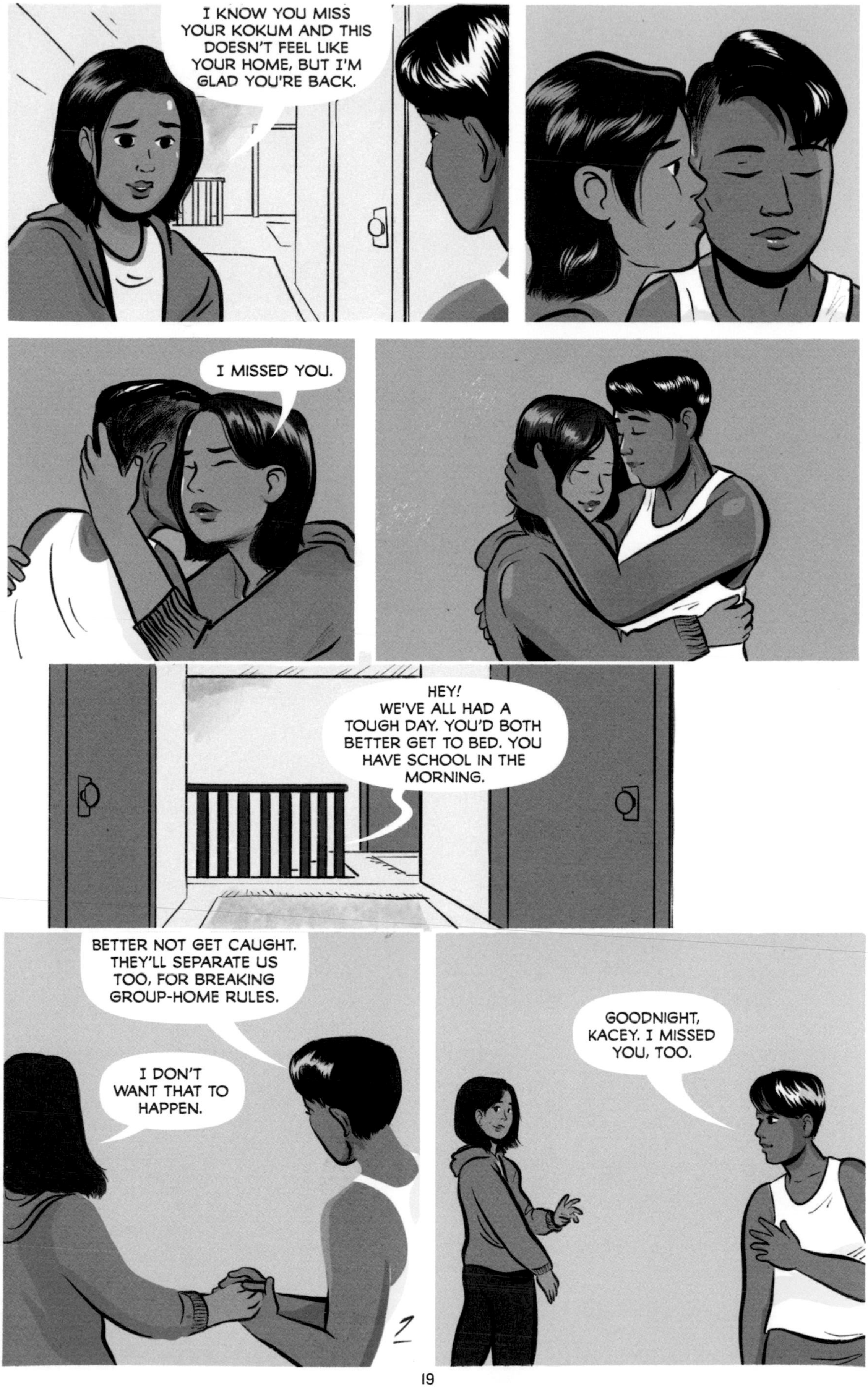
I KNOW YOU MISS YOUR KOKUM AND THIS DOESN'T FEEL LIKE YOUR HOME, BUT I'M GLAD YOU'RE BACK.
I MISSED YOU.
HEY! WE'VE ALL HAD A TOUGH DAY. YOU'D BOTH BETTER GET TO BED. YOU HAVE SCHOOL IN THE MORNING.
BETTER NOT GET CAUGHT. THEY'LL SEPARATE US TOO, FOR BREAKING GROUP-HOME RULES.
I DON'T WANT THAT TO HAPPEN.
GOODNIGHT, KACEY. I MISSED YOU, TOO.

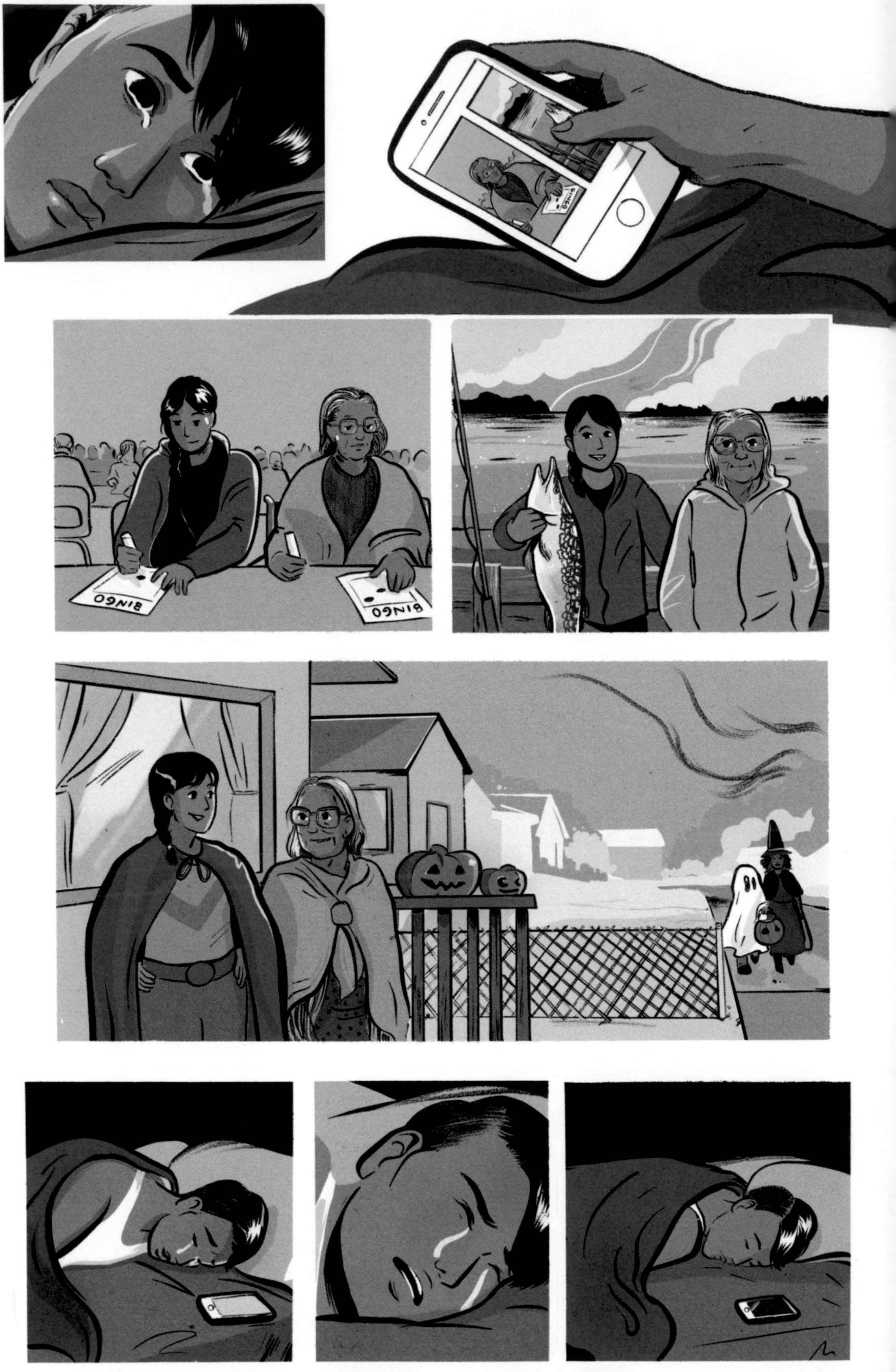
BINGO
BINGO
BINGO

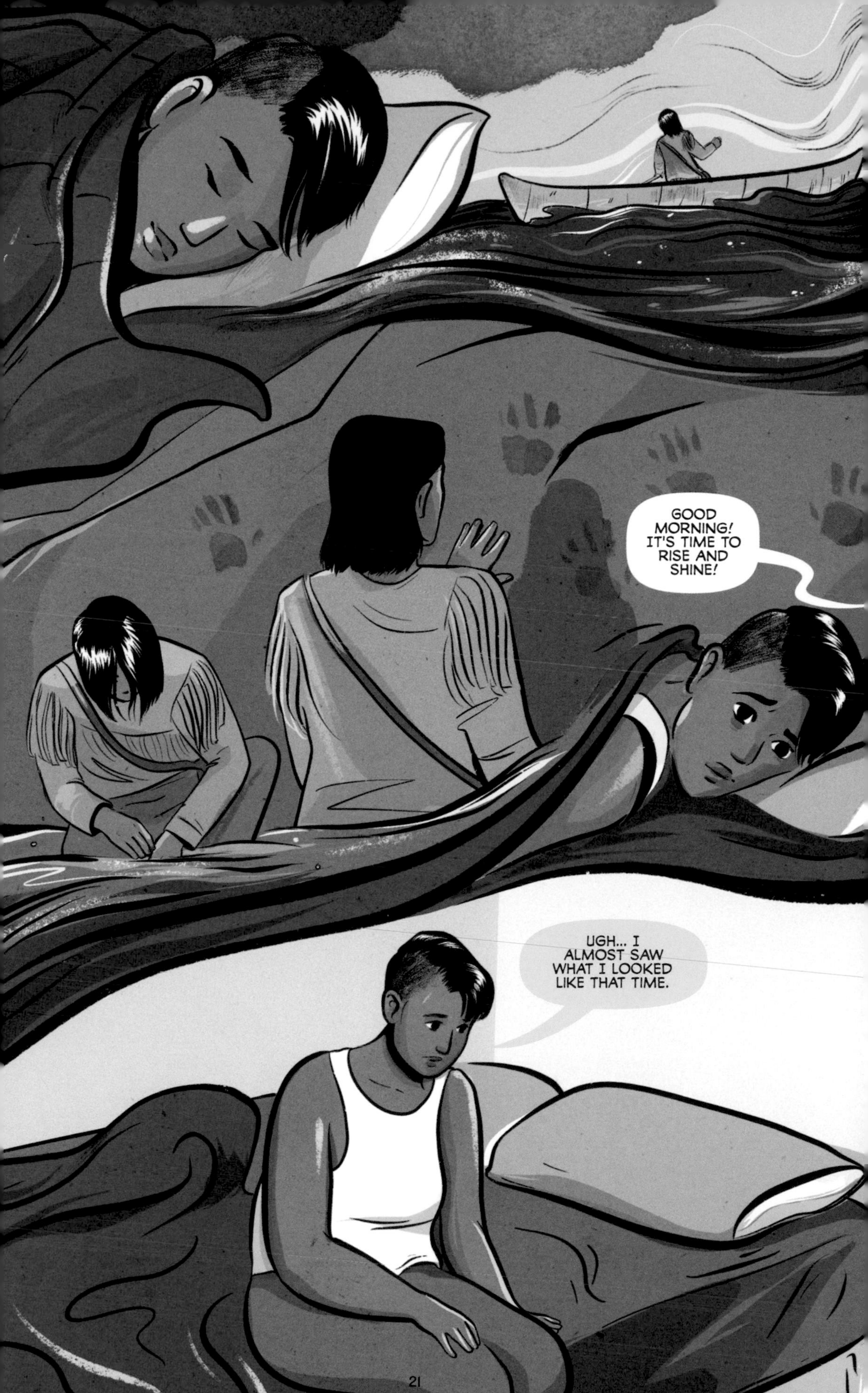
GOOD MORNING! IT'S TIME TO RISE AND SHINE!
UGH... I ALMOST SAW WHAT I LOOKED LIKE THAT TIME.

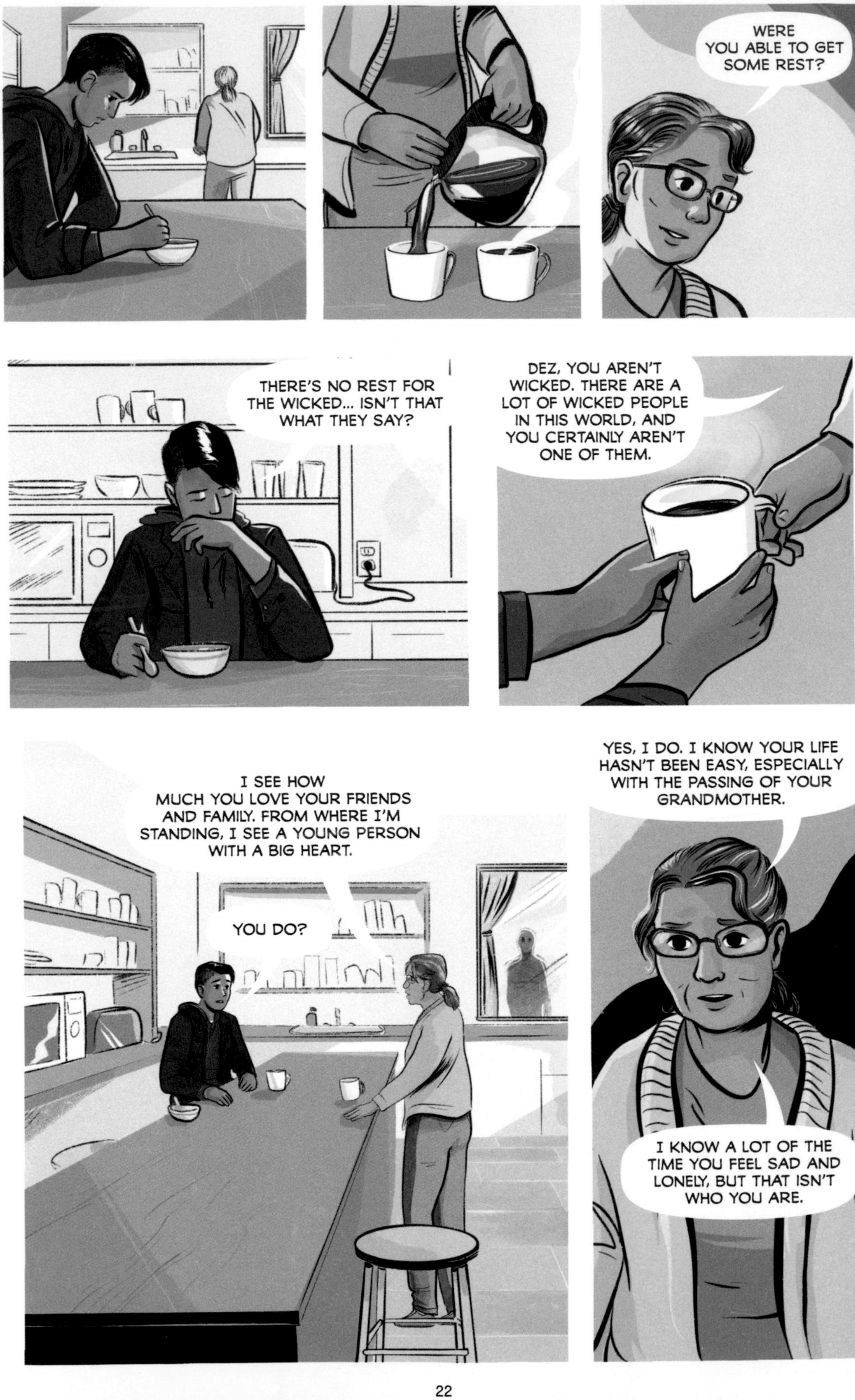
WERE YOU ABLE TO GET SOME REST?
THERE'S NO REST FOR THE WICKED... ISN'T THAT WHAT THEY SAY?
DEZ, YOU AREN'T WICKED. THERE ARE A LOT OF WICKED PEOPLE IN THIS WORLD, AND YOU CERTAINLY AREN'T ONE OF THEM.
I SEE HOW MUCH YOU LOVE YOUR FRIENDS AND FAMILY. FROM WHERE I'M STANDING, I SEE A YOUNG PERSON WITH A BIG HEART.
YOU DO?
YES, I DO. I KNOW YOUR LIFE HASN'T BEEN EASY, ESPECIALLY WITH THE PASSING OF YOUR GRANDMOTHER.
I KNOW A LOT OF THE TIME YOU FEEL SAD AND LONELY, BUT THAT ISN'T WHO YOU ARE.

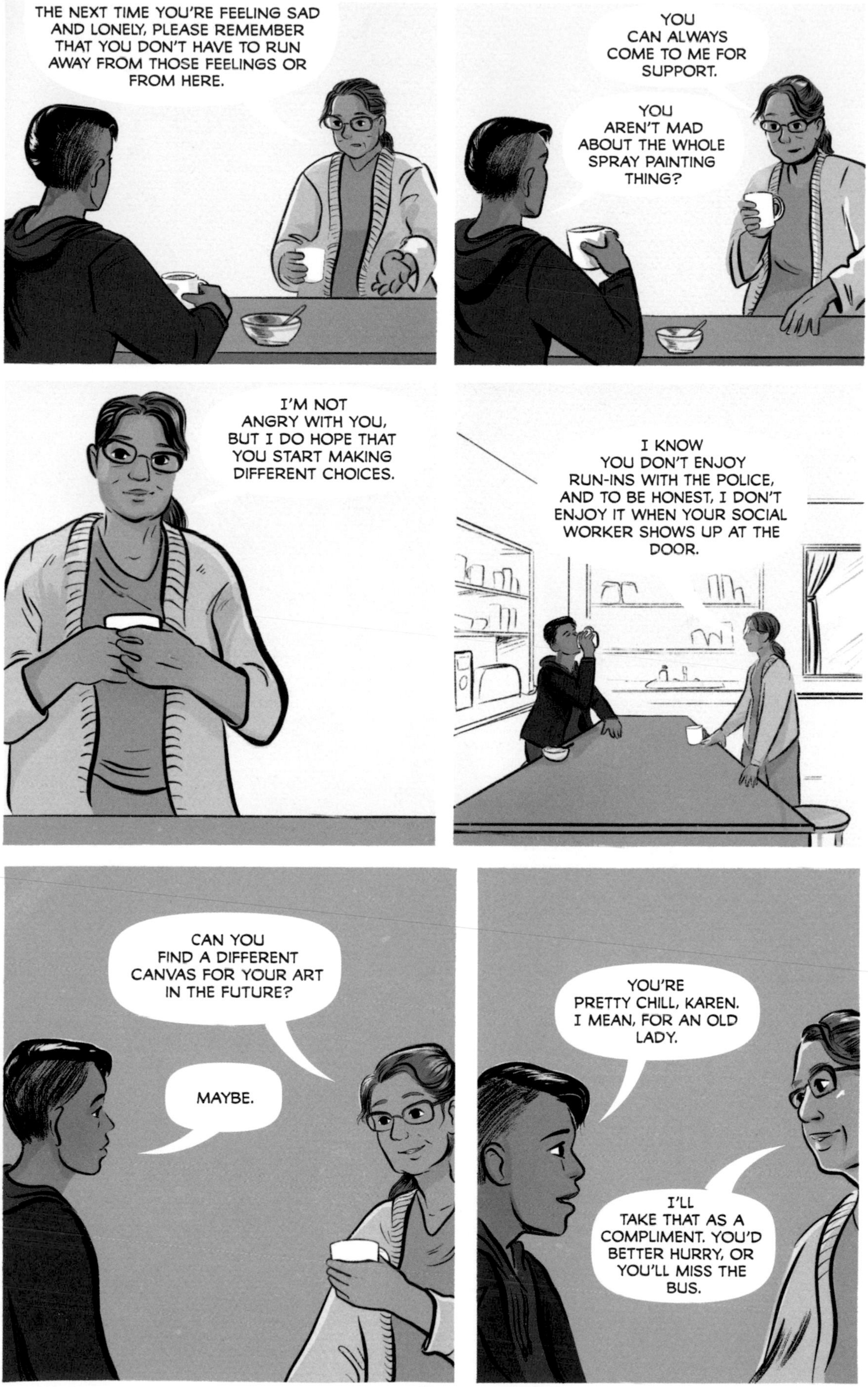
THE NEXT TIME YOU'RE FEELING SAD AND LONELY, PLEASE REMEMBER THAT YOU DON'T HAVE TO RUN AWAY FROM THOSE FEELINGS OR FROM HERE.
YOU CAN ALWAYS COME TO ME FOR SUPPORT.
YOU AREN'T MAD ABOUT THE WHOLE SPRAY PAINTING THING?
I'M NOT ANGRY WITH YOU, BUT I DO HOPE THAT YOU START MAKING DIFFERENT CHOICES.
I KNOW YOU DON'T ENJOY RUN-INS WITH THE POLICE, AND TO BE HONEST, I DON'T ENJOY IT WHEN YOUR SOCIAL WORKER SHOWS UP AT THE DOOR.
CAN YOU FIND A DIFFERENT CANVAS FOR YOUR ART IN THE FUTURE?
MAYBE.
YOU'RE PRETTY CHILL, KAREN. I MEAN, FOR AN OLD LADY.
I'LL TAKE THAT AS A COMPLIMENT. YOU'D BETTER HURRY, OR YOU'LL MISS THE BUS.

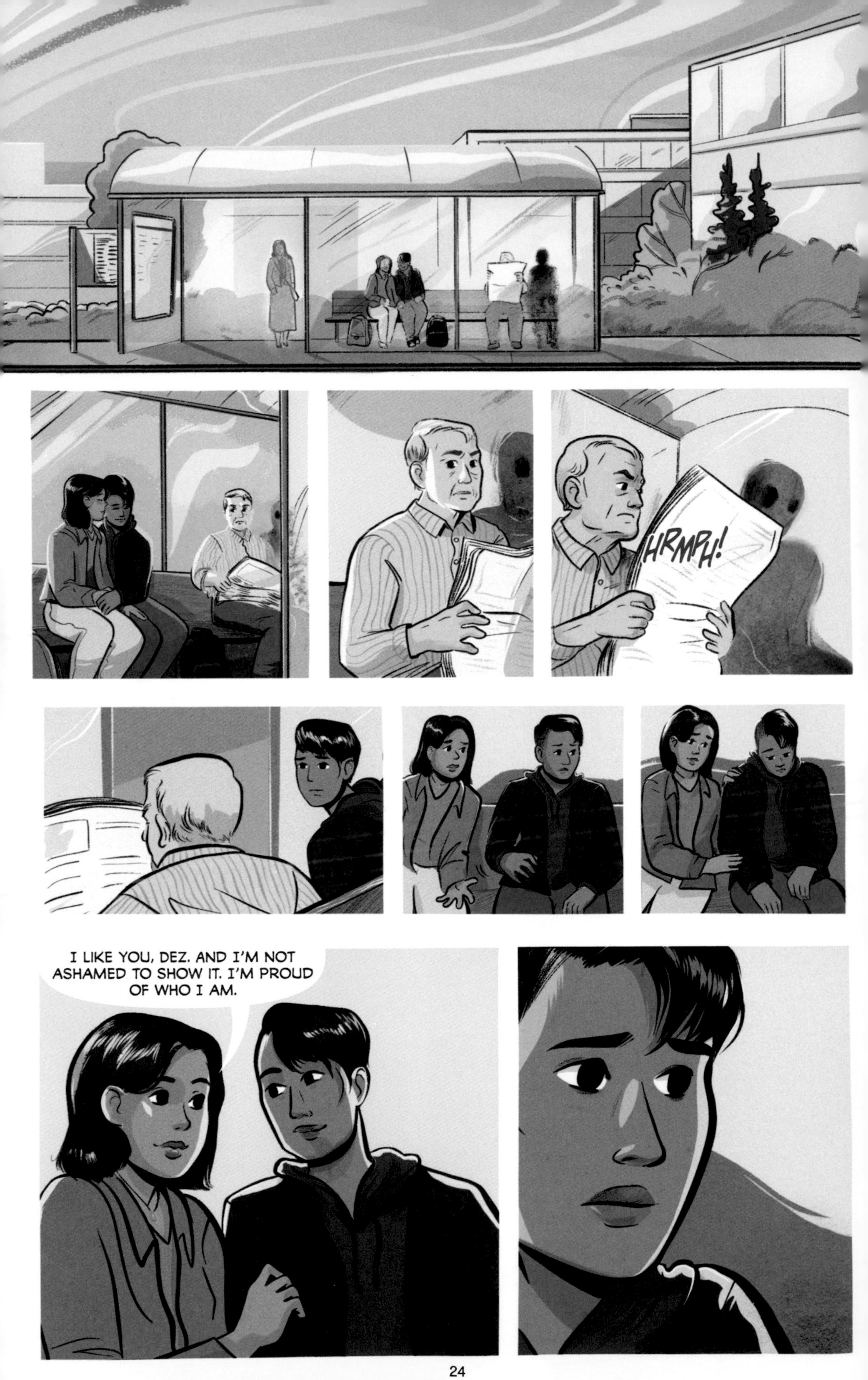
HRMPH!
I LIKE YOU, DEZ. AND I'M NOT ASHAMED TO SHOW IT. I'M PROUD OF WHO I AM.

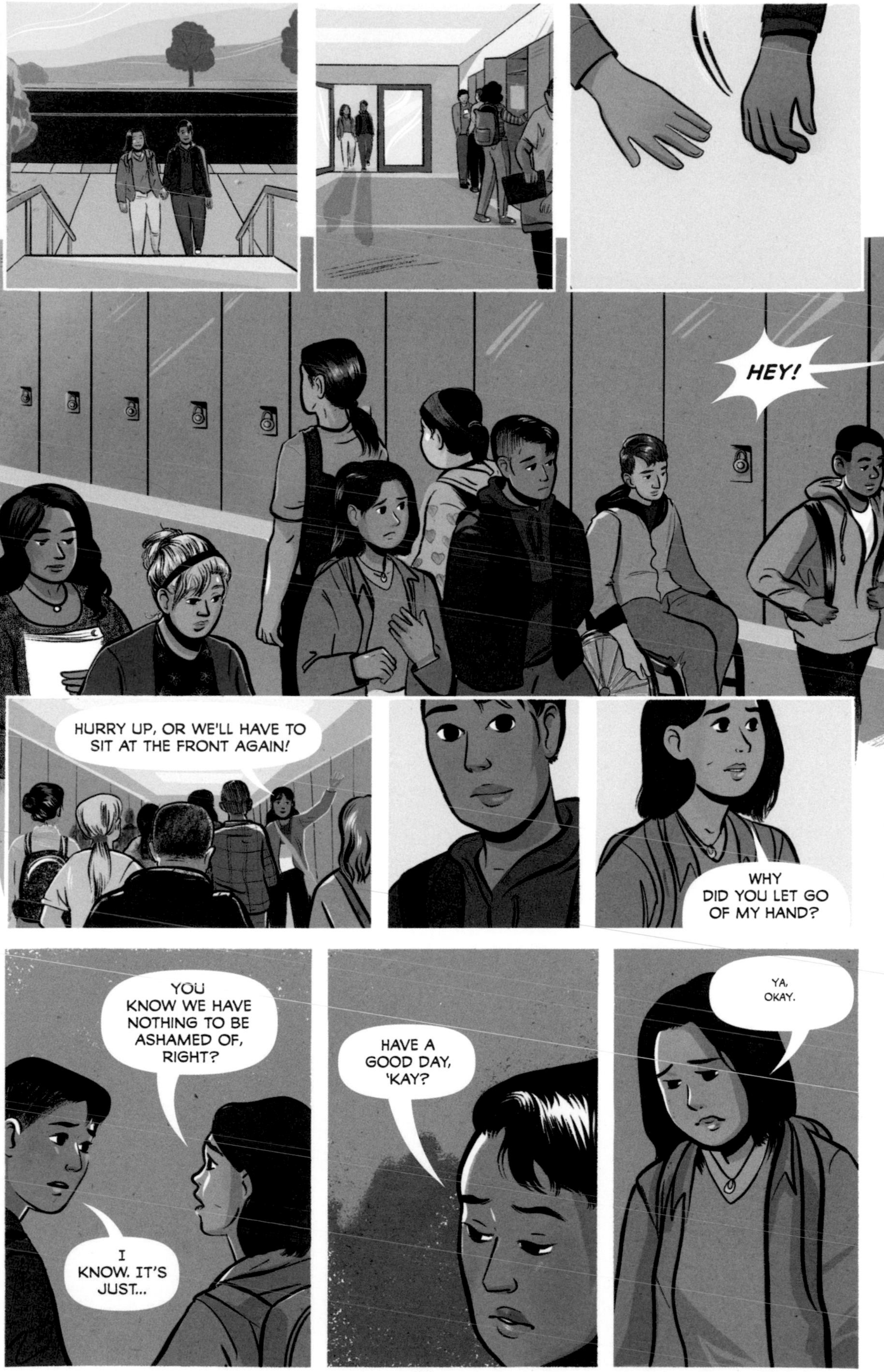
HEY!
HURRY UP, OR WE'LL HAVE TO SIT AT THE FRONT AGAIN!
WHY DID YOU LET GO OF MY HAND?
YOU KNOW WE HAVE NOTHING TO BE ASHAMED OF, RIGHT?
I KNOW. IT'S JUST...
HAVE A GOOD DAY, 'KAY?
YA, OKAY.

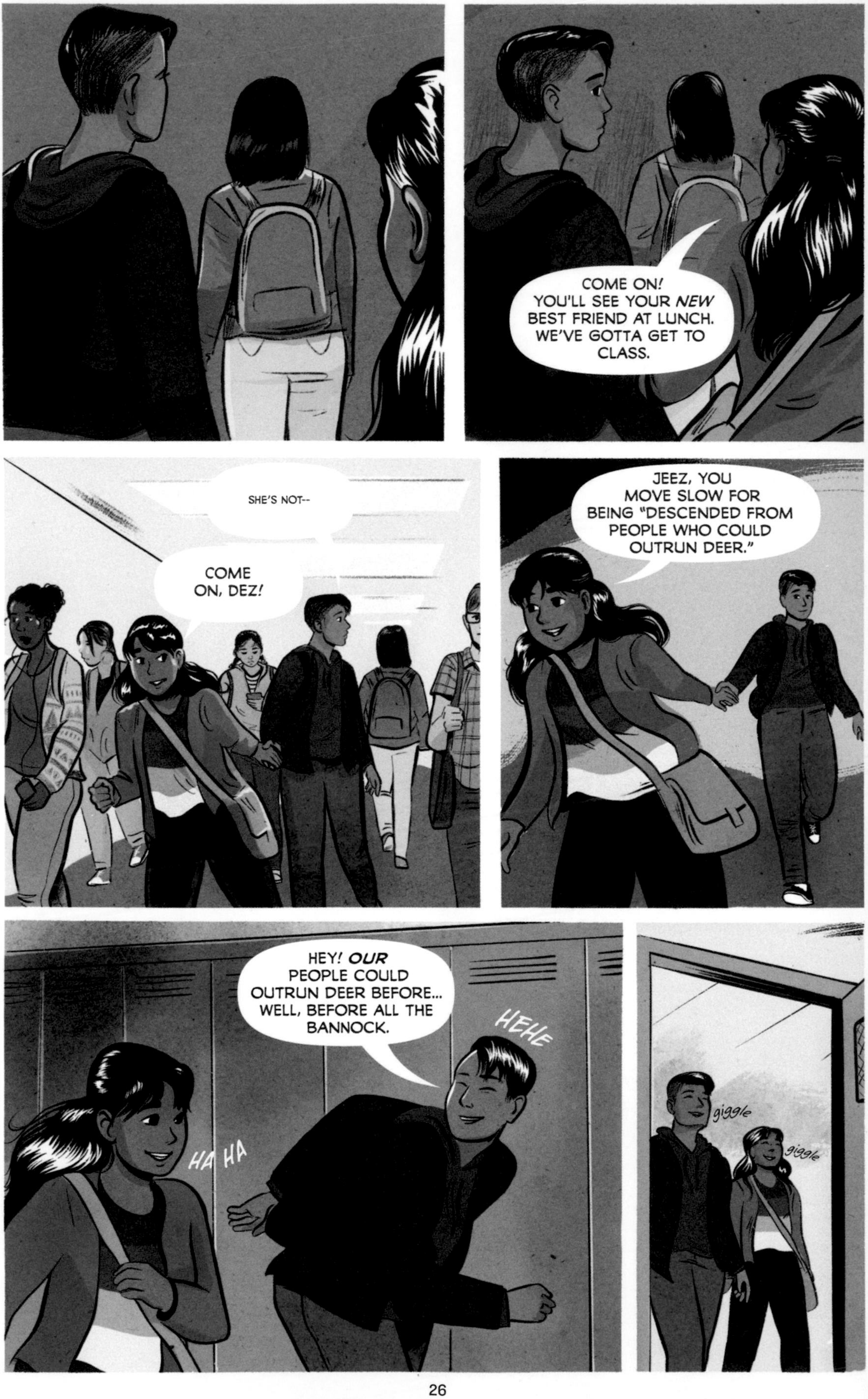
COME ON! YOU'LL SEE YOUR *NEW* BEST FRIEND AT LUNCH. WE'VE GOTTA GET TO CLASS.
SHE'S NOT--
COME ON, DEZ!
JEEZ, YOU MOVE SLOW FOR BEING "DESCENDED FROM PEOPLE WHO COULD OUTRUN DEER."
HEY! ***OUR*** PEOPLE COULD OUTRUN DEER BEFORE... WELL, BEFORE ALL THE BANNOCK.
HEHE
HA HA
giggle
giggle

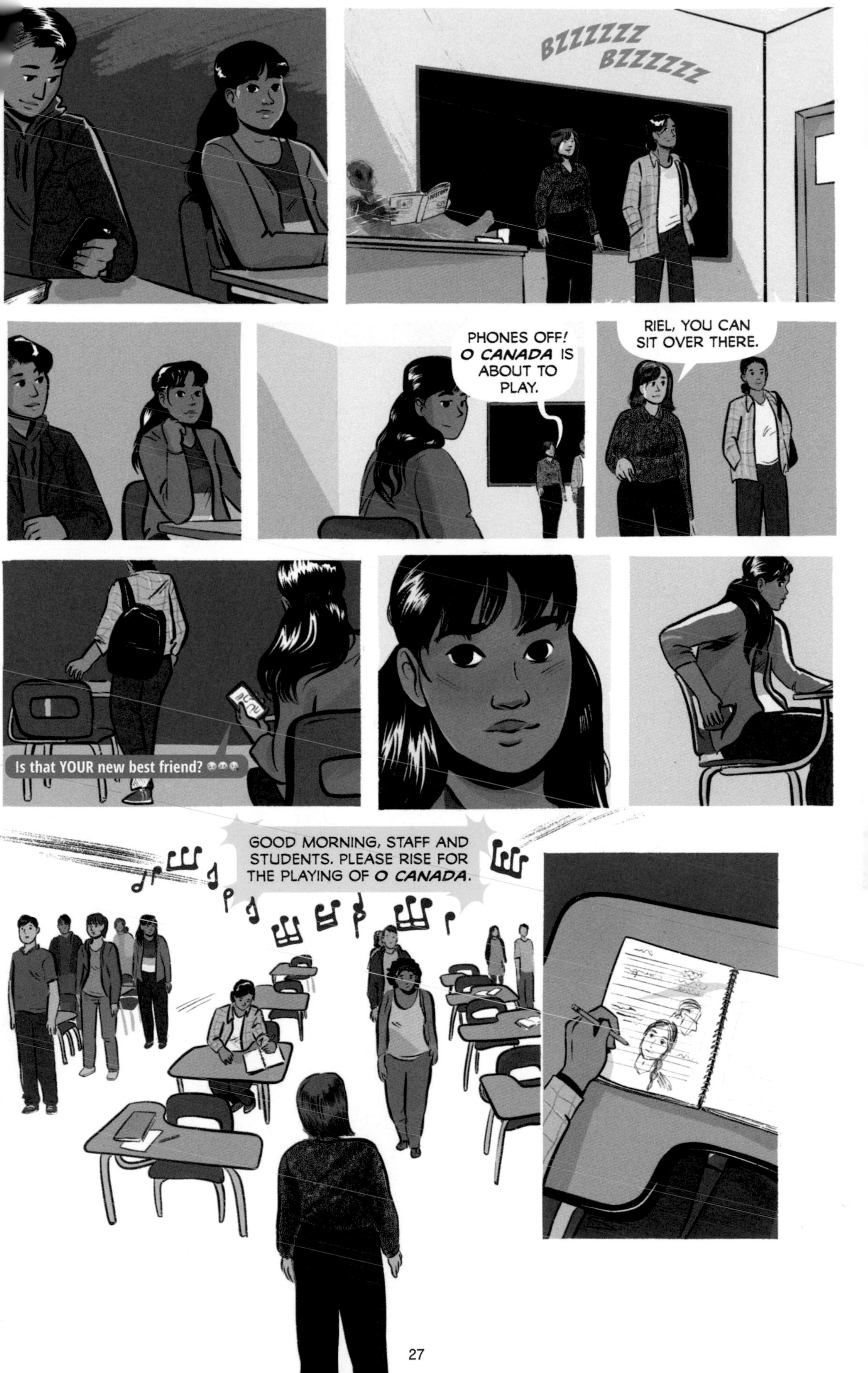
BZZZZZZ
BZZZZZZ
PHONES OFF! *O CANADA* IS ABOUT TO PLAY.
RIEL, YOU CAN SIT OVER THERE.
Is that YOUR new best friend?
GOOD MORNING, STAFF AND STUDENTS. PLEASE RISE FOR THE PLAYING OF *O CANADA*.

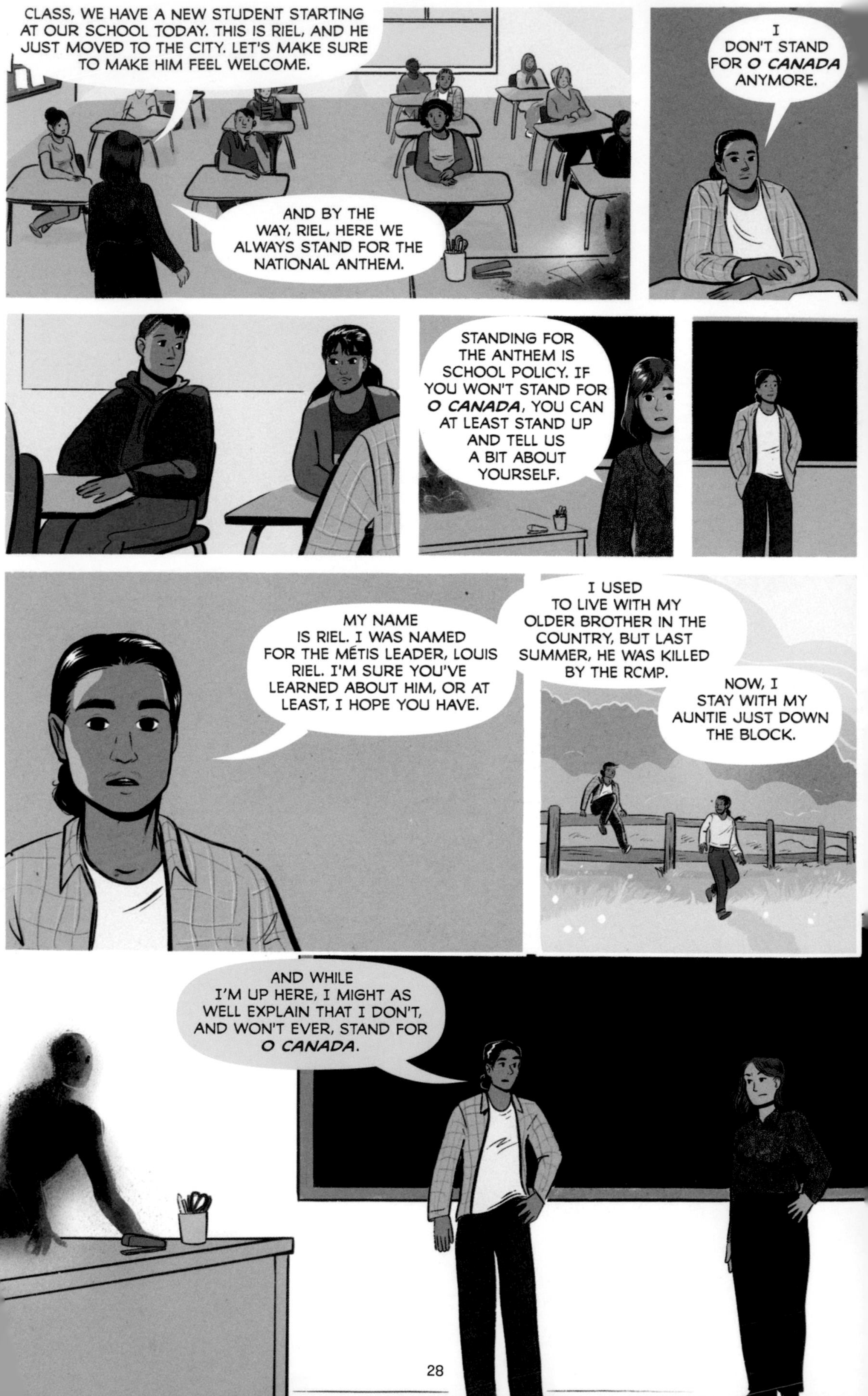
CLASS, WE HAVE A NEW STUDENT STARTING AT OUR SCHOOL TODAY. THIS IS RIEL, AND HE JUST MOVED TO THE CITY. LET'S MAKE SURE TO MAKE HIM FEEL WELCOME.
AND BY THE WAY, RIEL, HERE WE ALWAYS STAND FOR THE NATIONAL ANTHEM.
I DON'T STAND FOR *O CANADA* ANYMORE.
STANDING FOR THE ANTHEM IS SCHOOL POLICY. IF YOU WON'T STAND FOR *O CANADA*, YOU CAN AT LEAST STAND UP AND TELL US A BIT ABOUT YOURSELF.
MY NAME IS RIEL. I WAS NAMED FOR THE MÉTIS LEADER, LOUIS RIEL. I'M SURE YOU'VE LEARNED ABOUT HIM, OR AT LEAST, I HOPE YOU HAVE.
I USED TO LIVE WITH MY OLDER BROTHER IN THE COUNTRY, BUT LAST SUMMER, HE WAS KILLED BY THE RCMP.
NOW, I STAY WITH MY AUNTIE JUST DOWN THE BLOCK.
AND WHILE I'M UP HERE, I MIGHT AS WELL EXPLAIN THAT I DON'T, AND WON'T EVER, STAND FOR *O CANADA*.

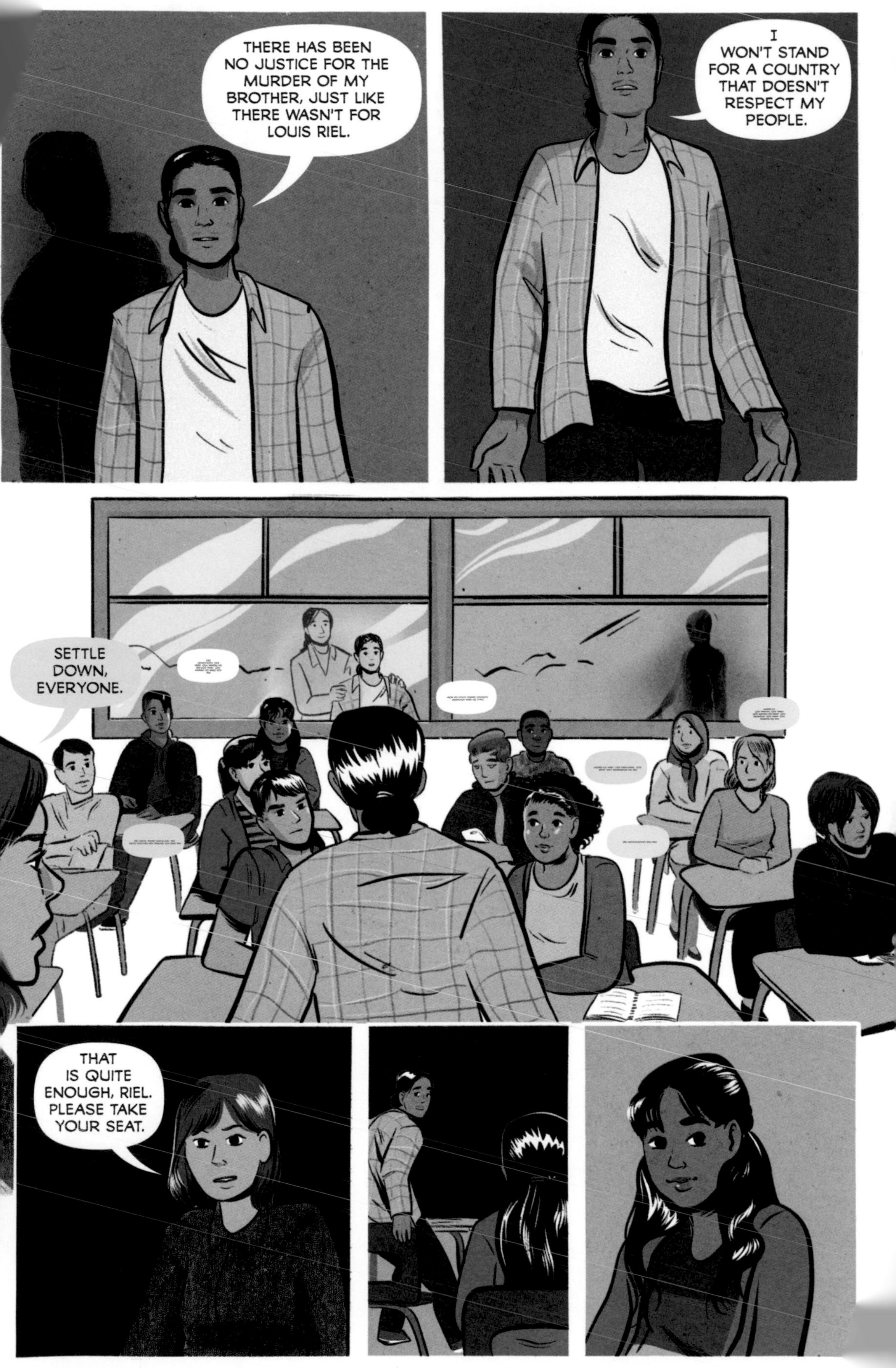
THERE HAS BEEN NO JUSTICE FOR THE MURDER OF MY BROTHER, JUST LIKE THERE WASN'T FOR LOUIS RIEL.
I WON'T STAND FOR A COUNTRY THAT DOESN'T RESPECT MY PEOPLE.
SETTLE DOWN, EVERYONE.
THAT IS QUITE ENOUGH, RIEL. PLEASE TAKE YOUR SEAT.

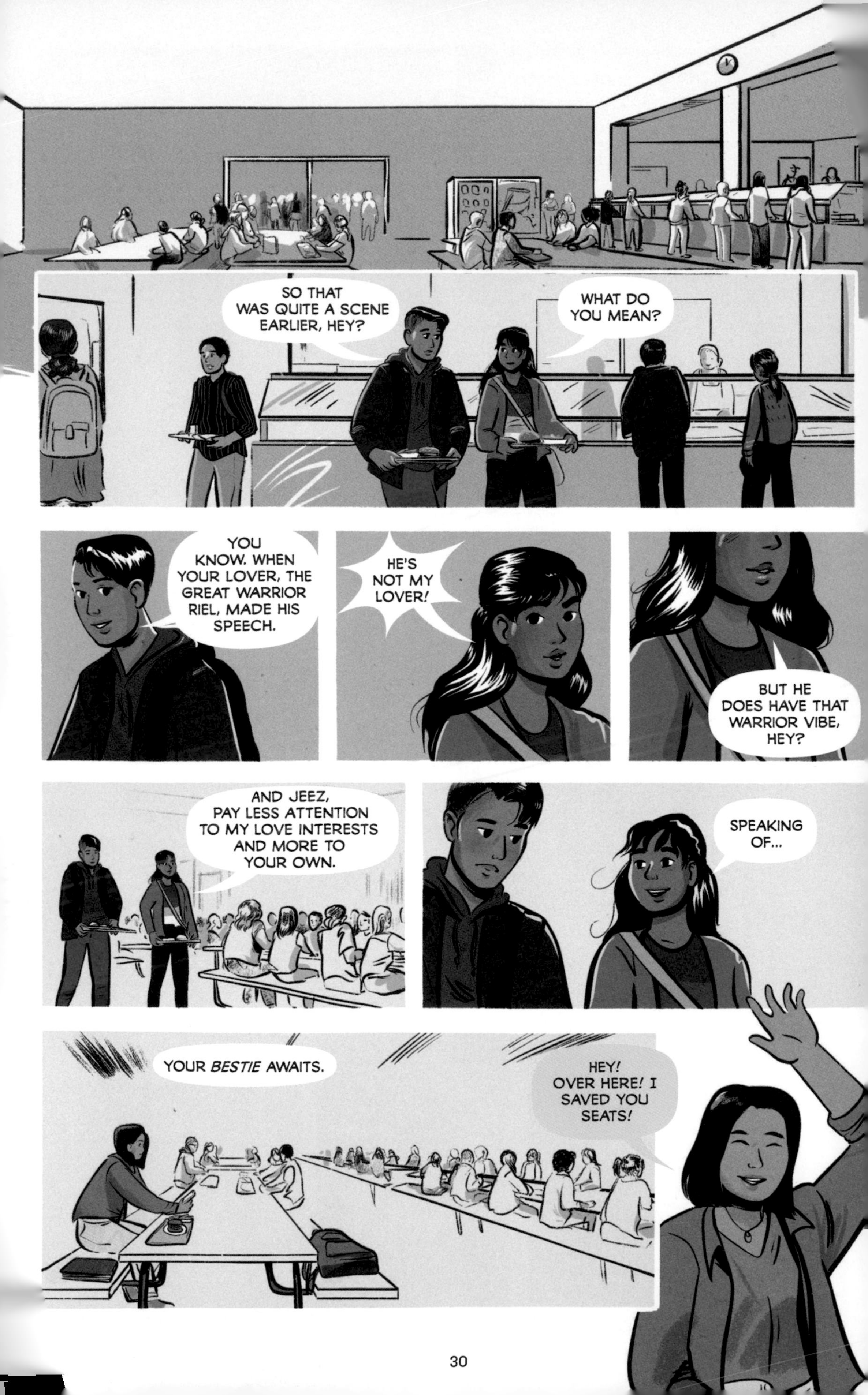
SO THAT WAS QUITE A SCENE EARLIER, HEY?
WHAT DO YOU MEAN?
YOU KNOW. WHEN YOUR LOVER, THE GREAT WARRIOR RIEL, MADE HIS SPEECH.
HE'S NOT MY LOVER!
BUT HE DOES HAVE THAT WARRIOR VIBE, HEY?
AND JEEZ, PAY LESS ATTENTION TO MY LOVE INTERESTS AND MORE TO YOUR OWN.
SPEAKING OF...
YOUR *BESTIE* AWAITS.
HEY! OVER HERE! I SAVED YOU SEATS!

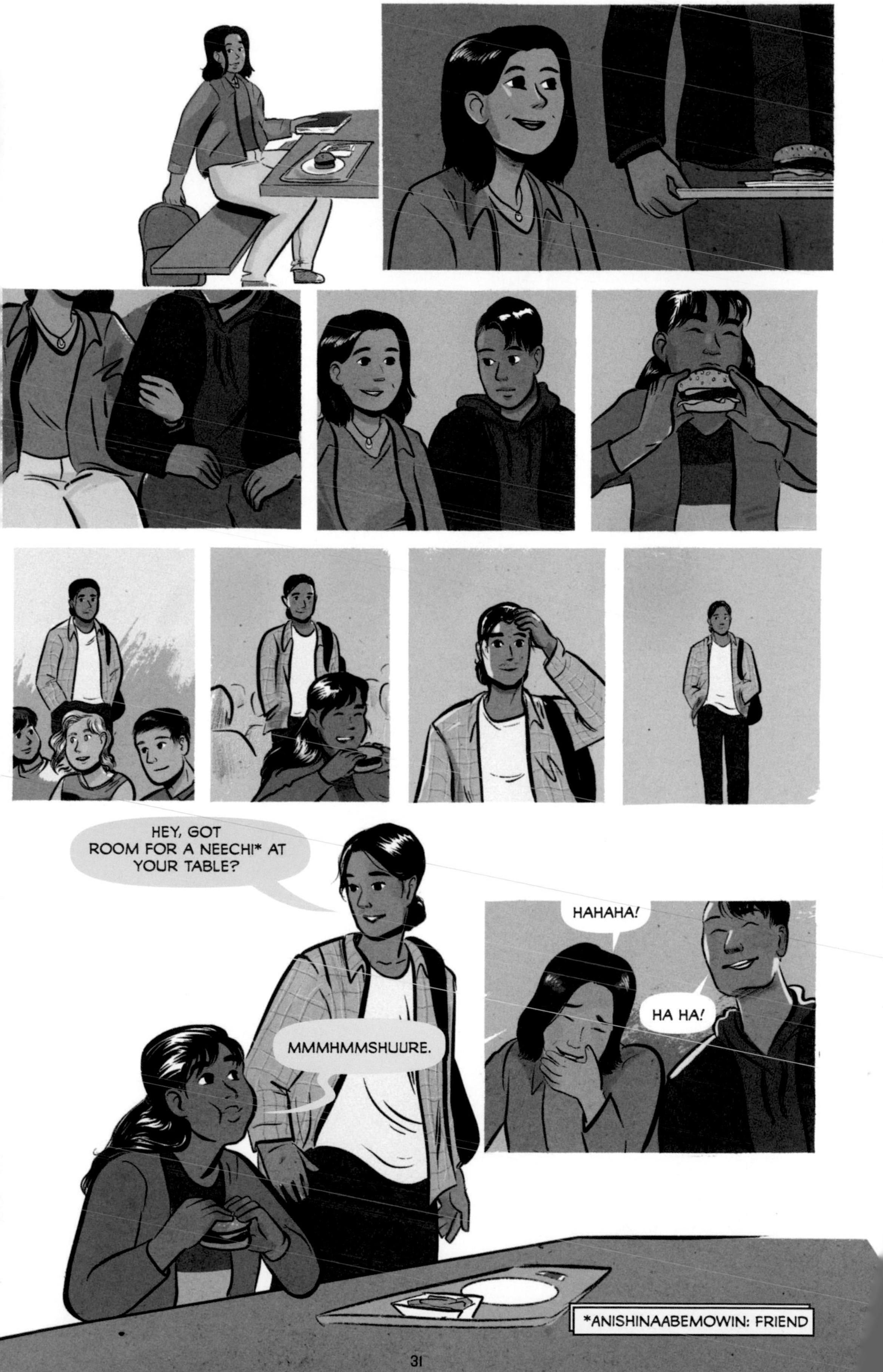
HEY, GOT ROOM FOR A NEECHI* AT YOUR TABLE?
MMMHMMSHUURE.
HAHAHA!
HA HA!
*ANISHINAABEMOWIN: FRIEND

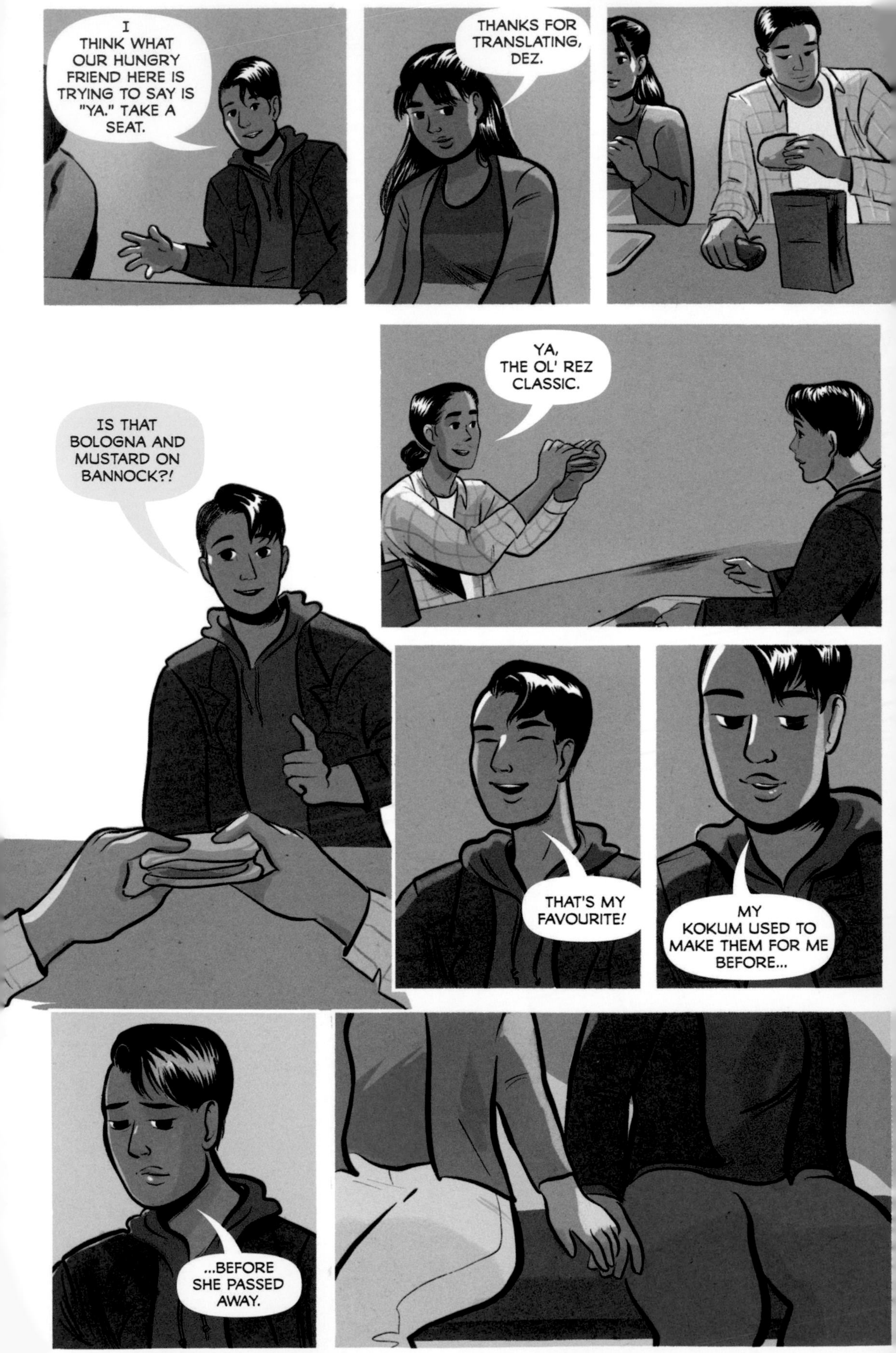
I THINK WHAT OUR HUNGRY FRIEND HERE IS TRYING TO SAY IS "YA." TAKE A SEAT.
THANKS FOR TRANSLATING, DEZ.
YA, THE OL' REZ CLASSIC.
IS THAT BOLOGNA AND MUSTARD ON BANNOCK?!
THAT'S MY FAVOURITE!
MY KOKUM USED TO MAKE THEM FOR ME BEFORE...
...BEFORE SHE PASSED AWAY.

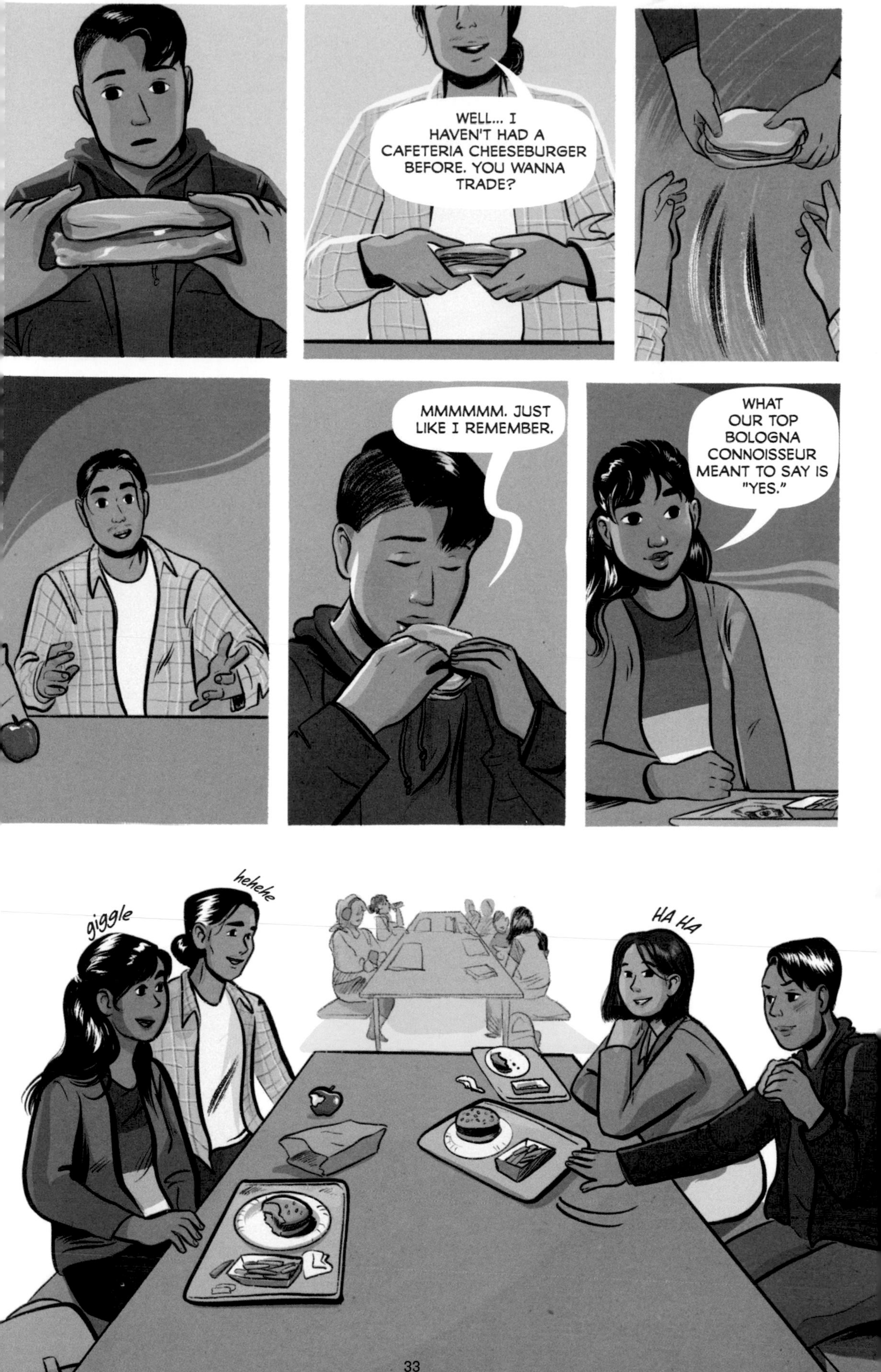
WELL... I HAVEN'T HAD A CAFETERIA CHEESEBURGER BEFORE. YOU WANNA TRADE?
MMMMMM. JUST LIKE I REMEMBER.
WHAT OUR TOP BOLOGNA CONNOISSEUR MEANT TO SAY IS "YES."
giggle
hehehe
HA HA

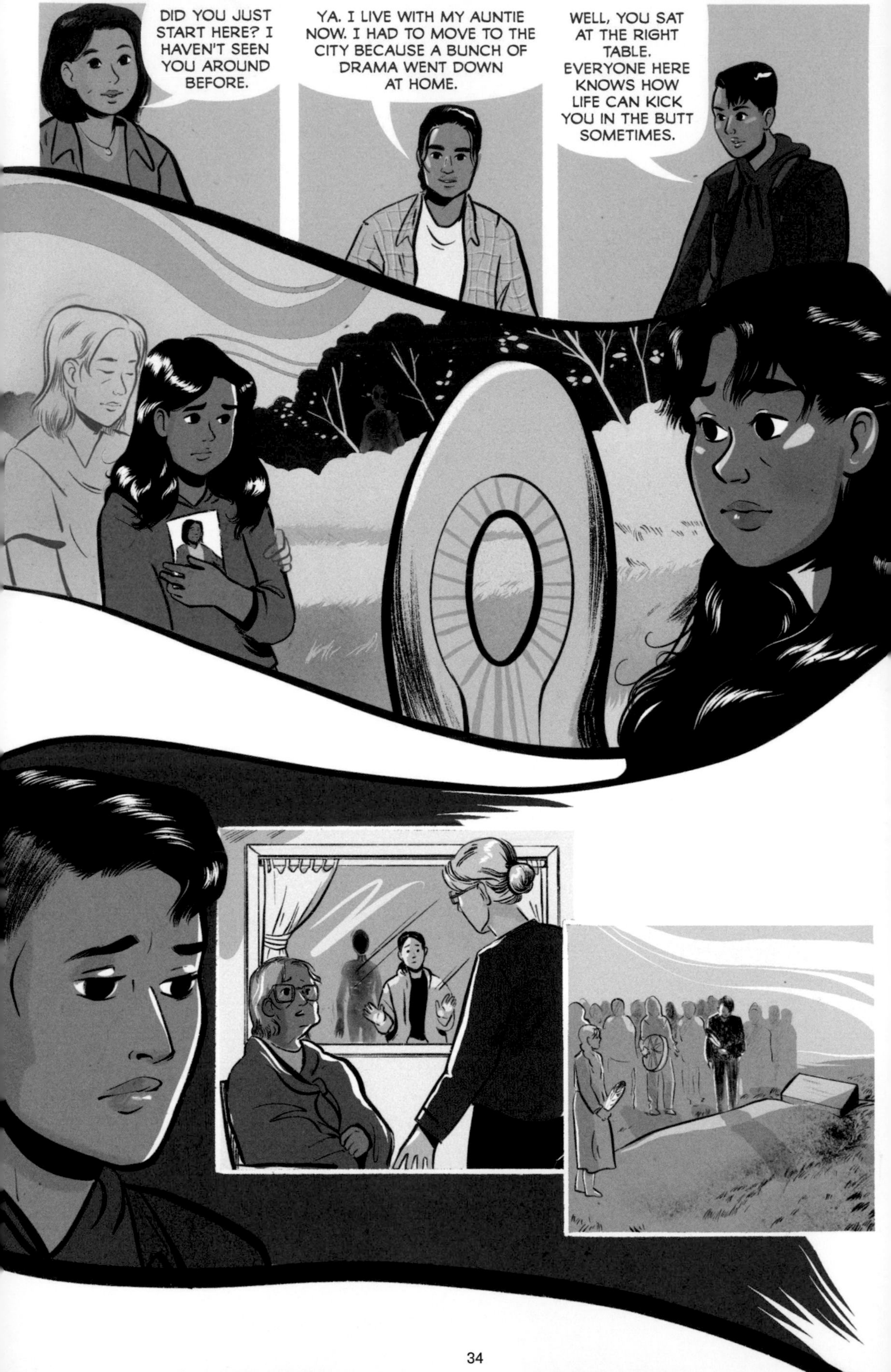
DID YOU JUST START HERE? I HAVEN'T SEEN YOU AROUND BEFORE.
YA. I LIVE WITH MY AUNTIE NOW. I HAD TO MOVE TO THE CITY BECAUSE A BUNCH OF DRAMA WENT DOWN AT HOME.
WELL, YOU SAT AT THE RIGHT TABLE. EVERYONE HERE KNOWS HOW LIFE CAN KICK YOU IN THE BUTT SOMETIMES.

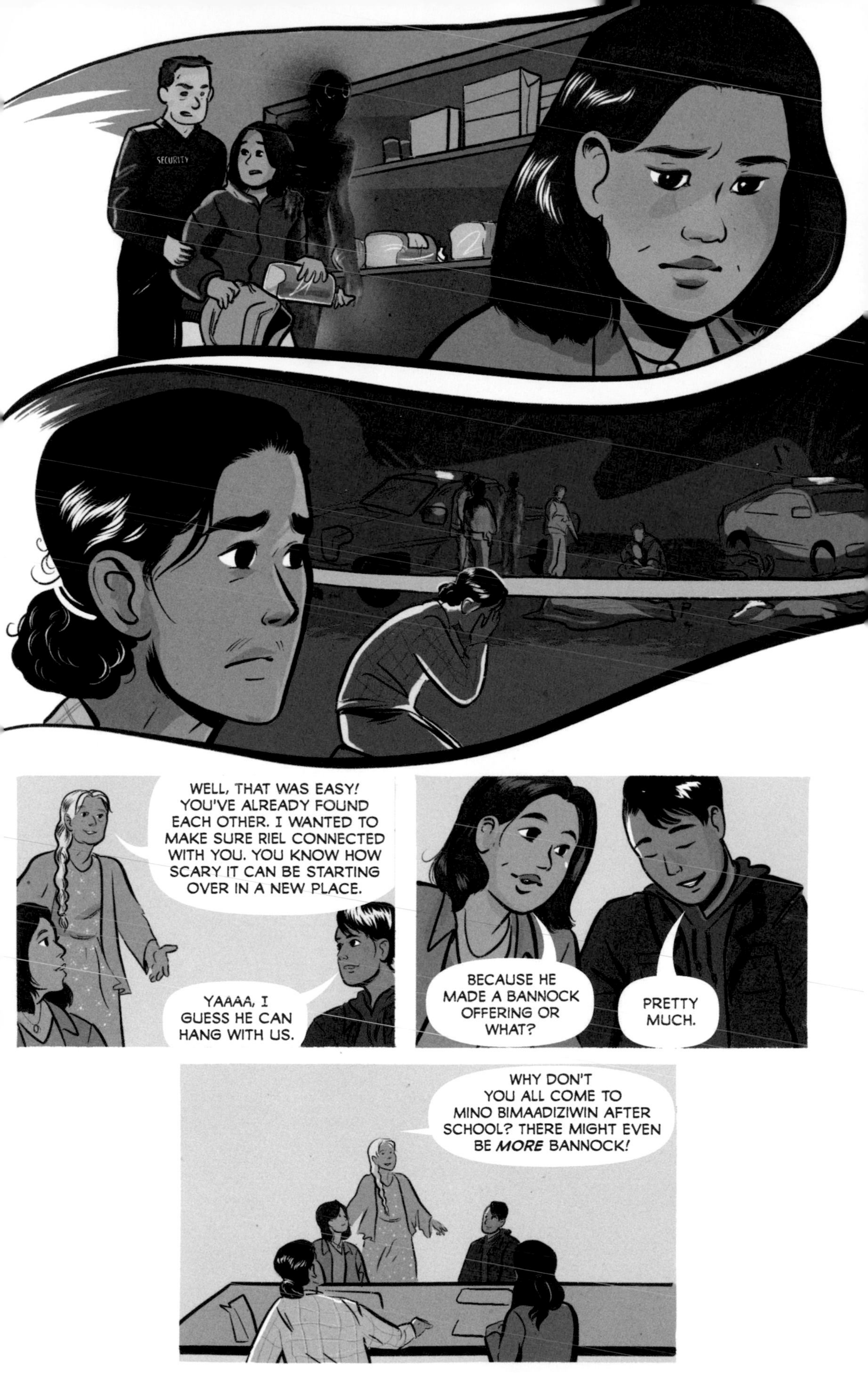
SECURITY
WELL, THAT WAS EASY! YOU'VE ALREADY FOUND EACH OTHER. I WANTED TO MAKE SURE RIEL CONNECTED WITH YOU. YOU KNOW HOW SCARY IT CAN BE STARTING OVER IN A NEW PLACE.
YAAAA, I GUESS HE CAN HANG WITH US.
BECAUSE HE MADE A BANNOCK OFFERING OR WHAT?
PRETTY MUCH.
WHY DON'T YOU ALL COME TO MINO BIMAADIZIWIN AFTER SCHOOL? THERE MIGHT EVEN BE *MORE* BANNOCK!

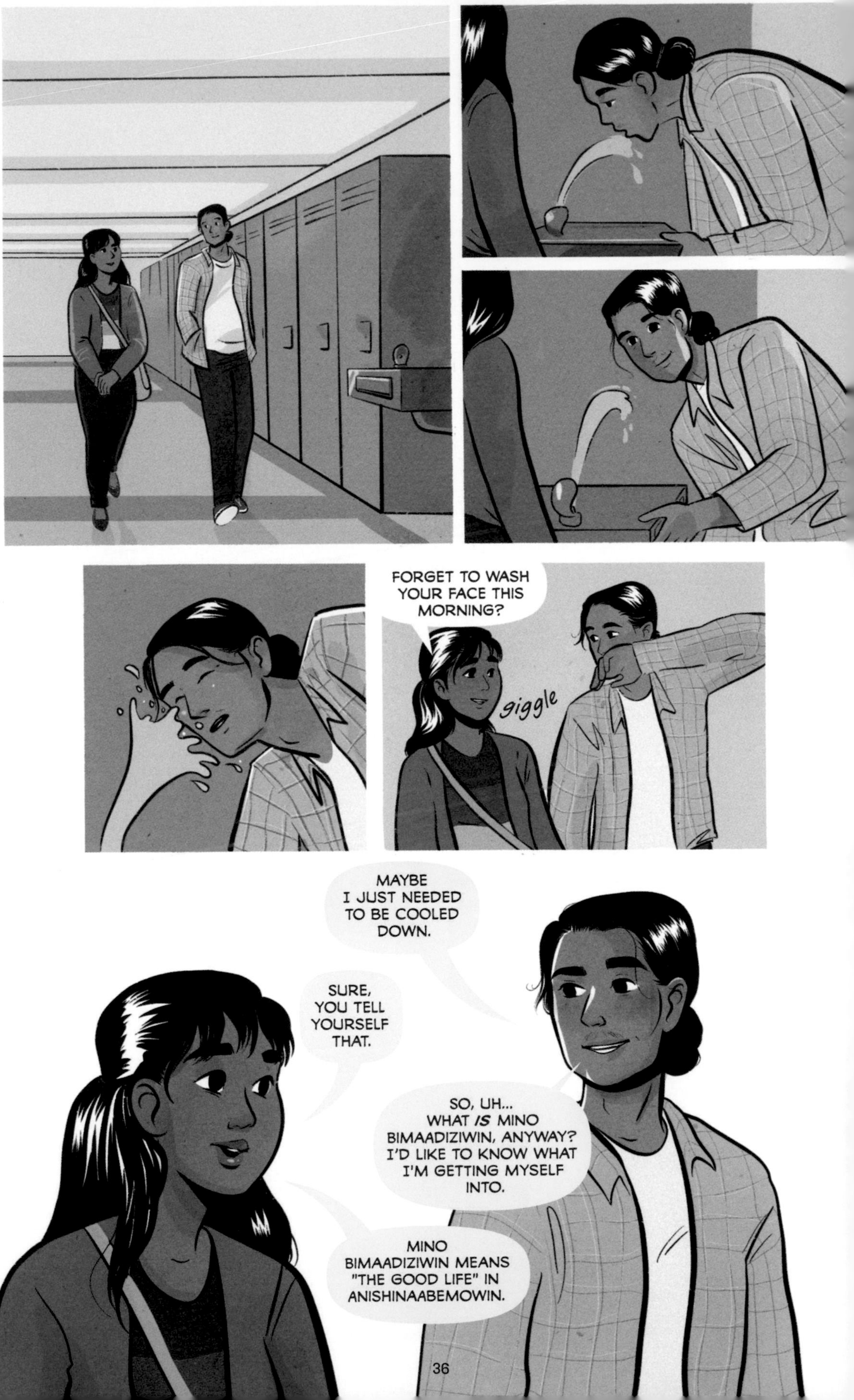

FORGET TO WASH YOUR FACE THIS MORNING?
giggle
MAYBE I JUST NEEDED TO BE COOLED DOWN.
SURE, YOU TELL YOURSELF THAT.
SO, UH... WHAT *IS* MINO BIMAADIZIWIN, ANYWAY? I'D LIKE TO KNOW WHAT I'M GETTING MYSELF INTO.
MINO BIMAADIZIWIN MEANS "THE GOOD LIFE" IN ANISHINAABEMOWIN.

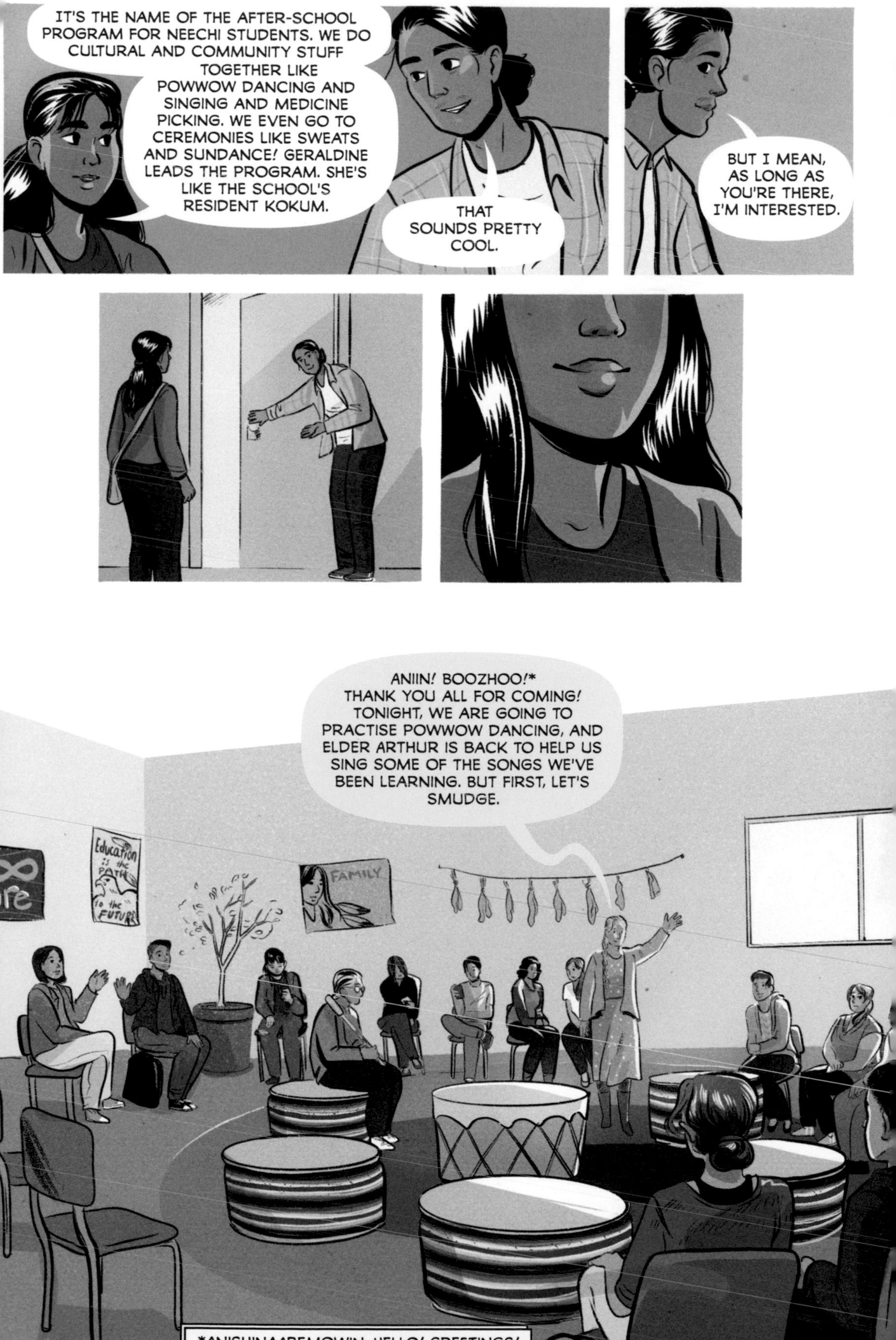
IT'S THE NAME OF THE AFTER-SCHOOL PROGRAM FOR NEECHI STUDENTS. WE DO CULTURAL AND COMMUNITY STUFF TOGETHER LIKE POWWOW DANCING AND SINGING AND MEDICINE PICKING. WE EVEN GO TO CEREMONIES LIKE SWEATS AND SUNDANCE! GERALDINE LEADS THE PROGRAM. SHE'S LIKE THE SCHOOL'S RESIDENT KOKUM.
THAT SOUNDS PRETTY COOL.
BUT I MEAN, AS LONG AS YOU'RE THERE, I'M INTERESTED.
ANIIN! BOOZHOO!* THANK YOU ALL FOR COMING! TONIGHT, WE ARE GOING TO PRACTISE POWWOW DANCING, AND ELDER ARTHUR IS BACK TO HELP US SING SOME OF THE SONGS WE'VE BEEN LEARNING. BUT FIRST, LET'S SMUDGE.
Education is the PATH to the FUTURE
FAMILY
*ANISHINAABEMOWIN: HELLO! GREETINGS!

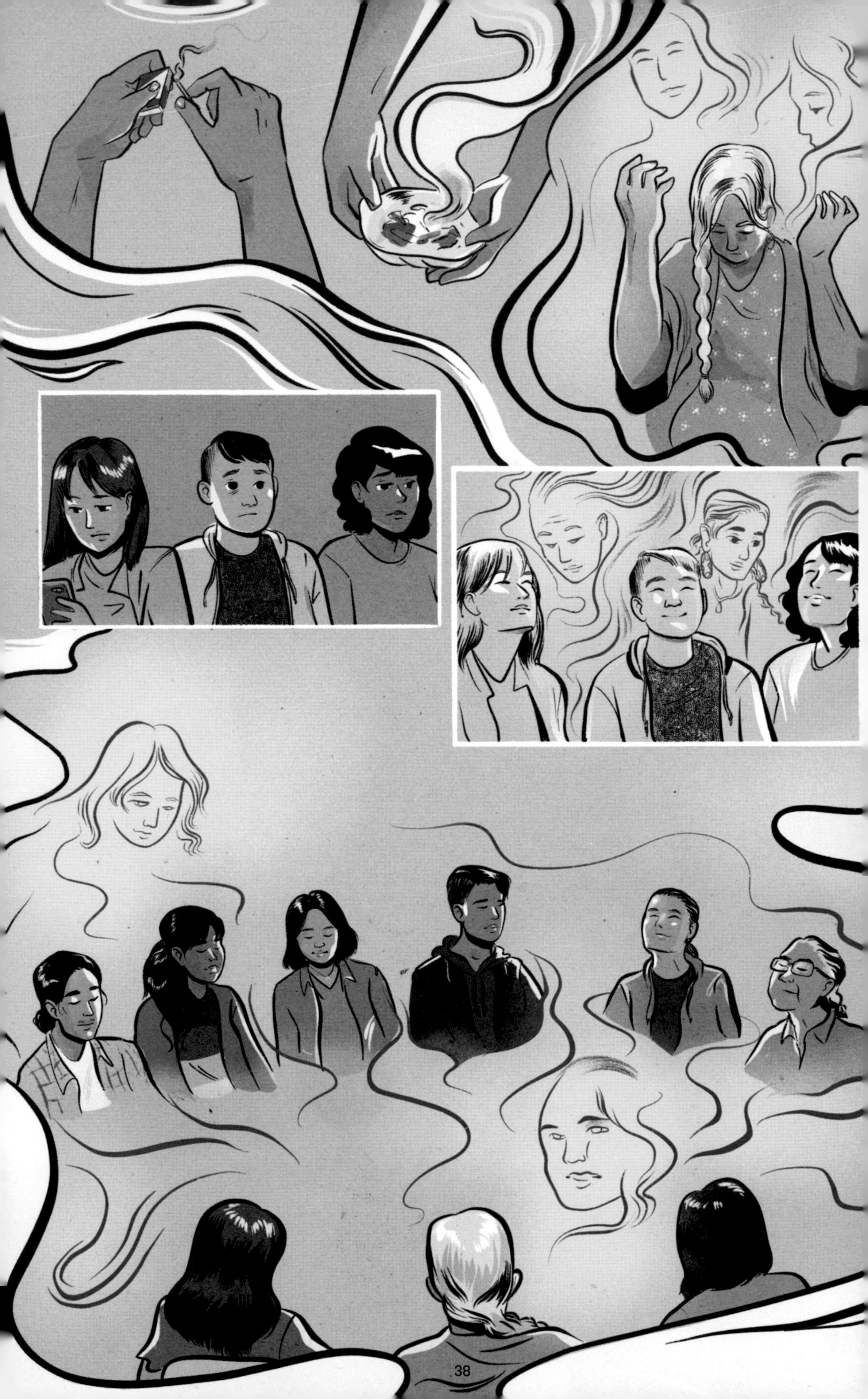

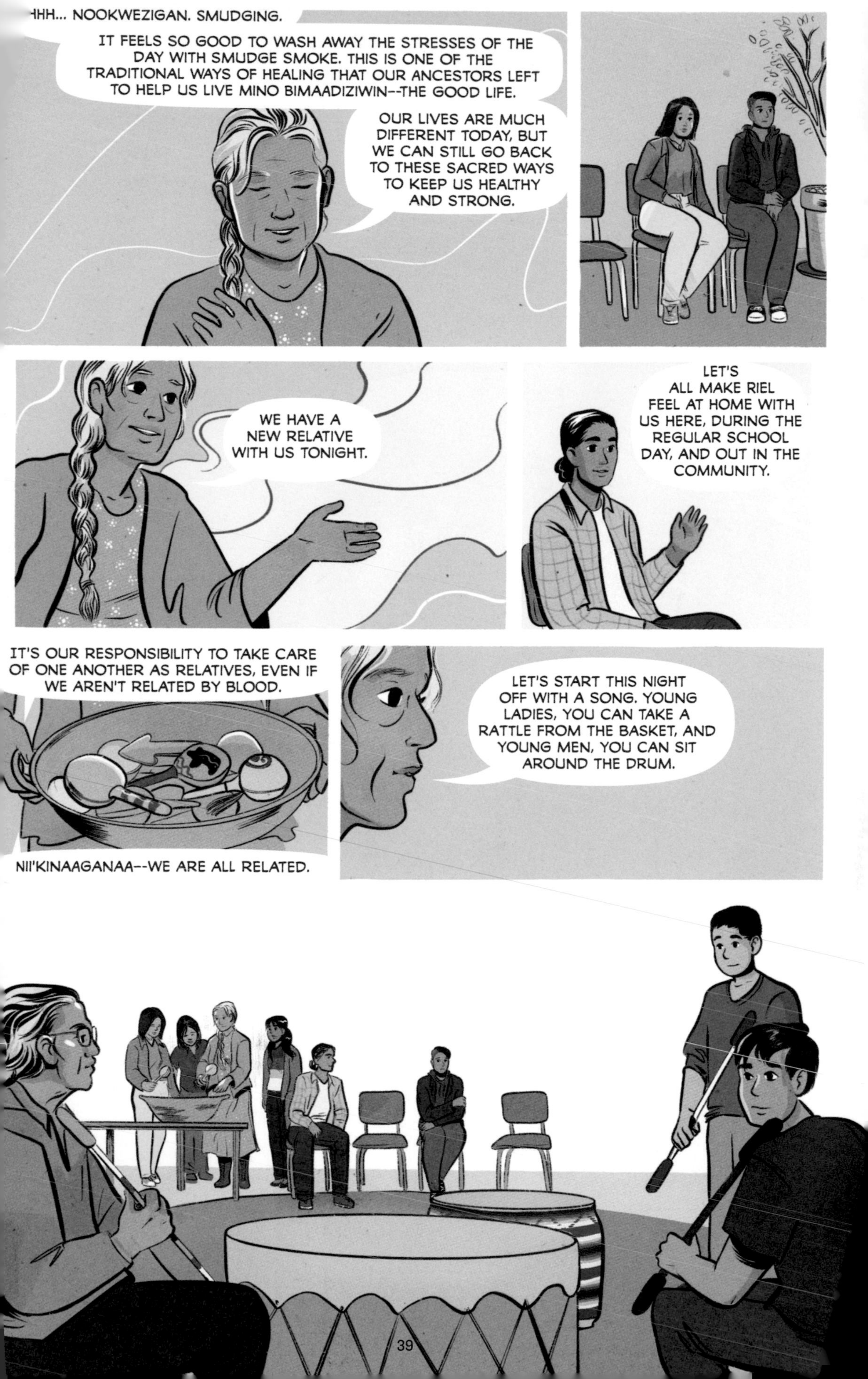
HHH... NOOKWEZIGAN. SMUDGING.
IT FEELS SO GOOD TO WASH AWAY THE STRESSES OF THE DAY WITH SMUDGE SMOKE. THIS IS ONE OF THE TRADITIONAL WAYS OF HEALING THAT OUR ANCESTORS LEFT TO HELP US LIVE MINO BIMAADIZIWIN--THE GOOD LIFE.
OUR LIVES ARE MUCH DIFFERENT TODAY, BUT WE CAN STILL GO BACK TO THESE SACRED WAYS TO KEEP US HEALTHY AND STRONG.
WE HAVE A NEW RELATIVE WITH US TONIGHT.
LET'S ALL MAKE RIEL FEEL AT HOME WITH US HERE, DURING THE REGULAR SCHOOL DAY, AND OUT IN THE COMMUNITY.
IT'S OUR RESPONSIBILITY TO TAKE CARE OF ONE ANOTHER AS RELATIVES, EVEN IF WE AREN'T RELATED BY BLOOD.
NII'KINAAGANAA--WE ARE ALL RELATED.
LET'S START THIS NIGHT OFF WITH A SONG. YOUNG LADIES, YOU CAN TAKE A RATTLE FROM THE BASKET, AND YOUNG MEN, YOU CAN SIT AROUND THE DRUM.

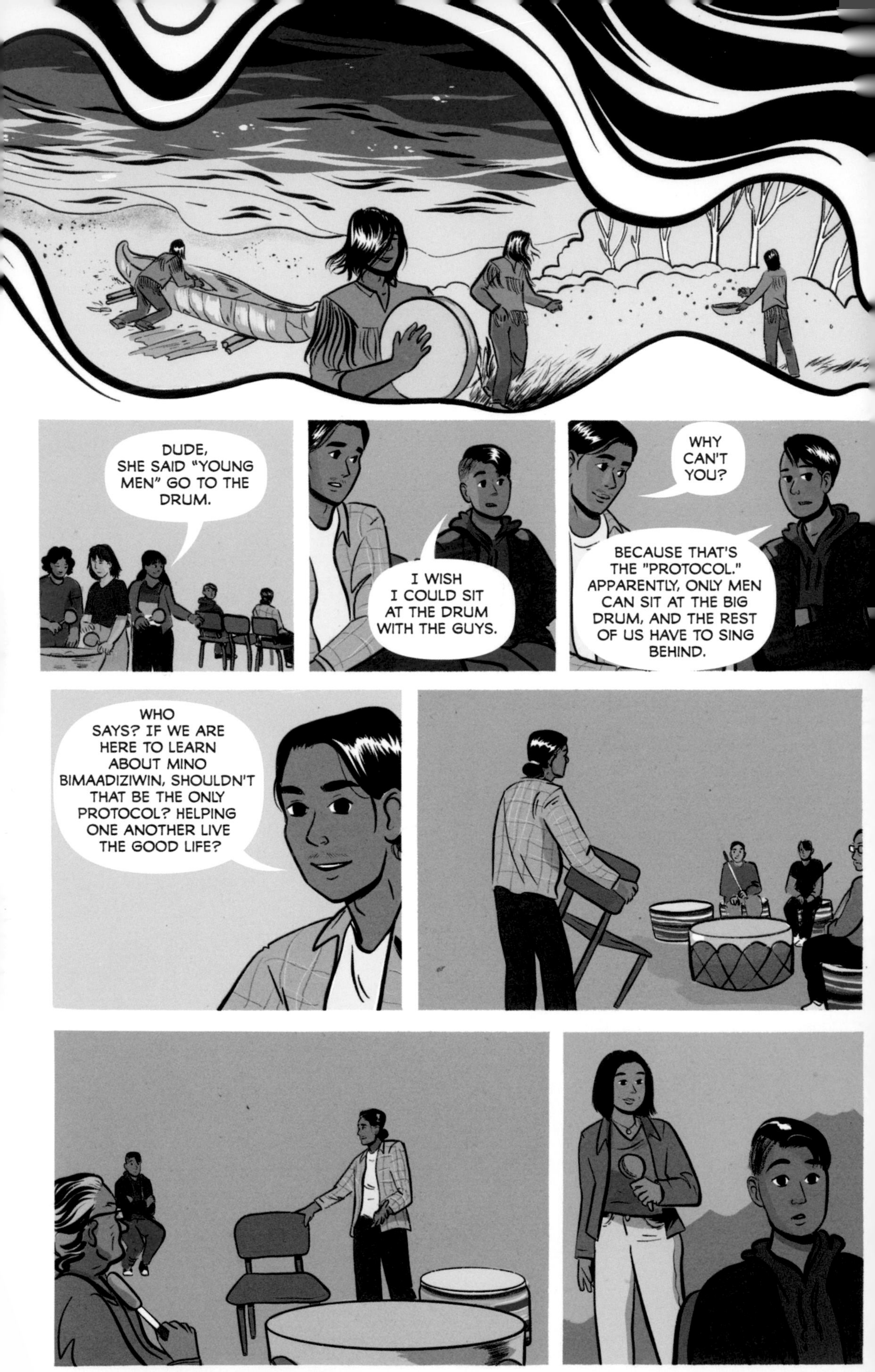
DUDE, SHE SAID "YOUNG MEN" GO TO THE DRUM.
I WISH I COULD SIT AT THE DRUM WITH THE GUYS.
WHY CAN'T YOU?
BECAUSE THAT'S THE "PROTOCOL." APPARENTLY, ONLY MEN CAN SIT AT THE BIG DRUM, AND THE REST OF US HAVE TO SING BEHIND.
WHO SAYS? IF WE ARE HERE TO LEARN ABOUT MINO BIMAADIZIWIN, SHOULDN'T THAT BE THE ONLY PROTOCOL? HELPING ONE ANOTHER LIVE THE GOOD LIFE?

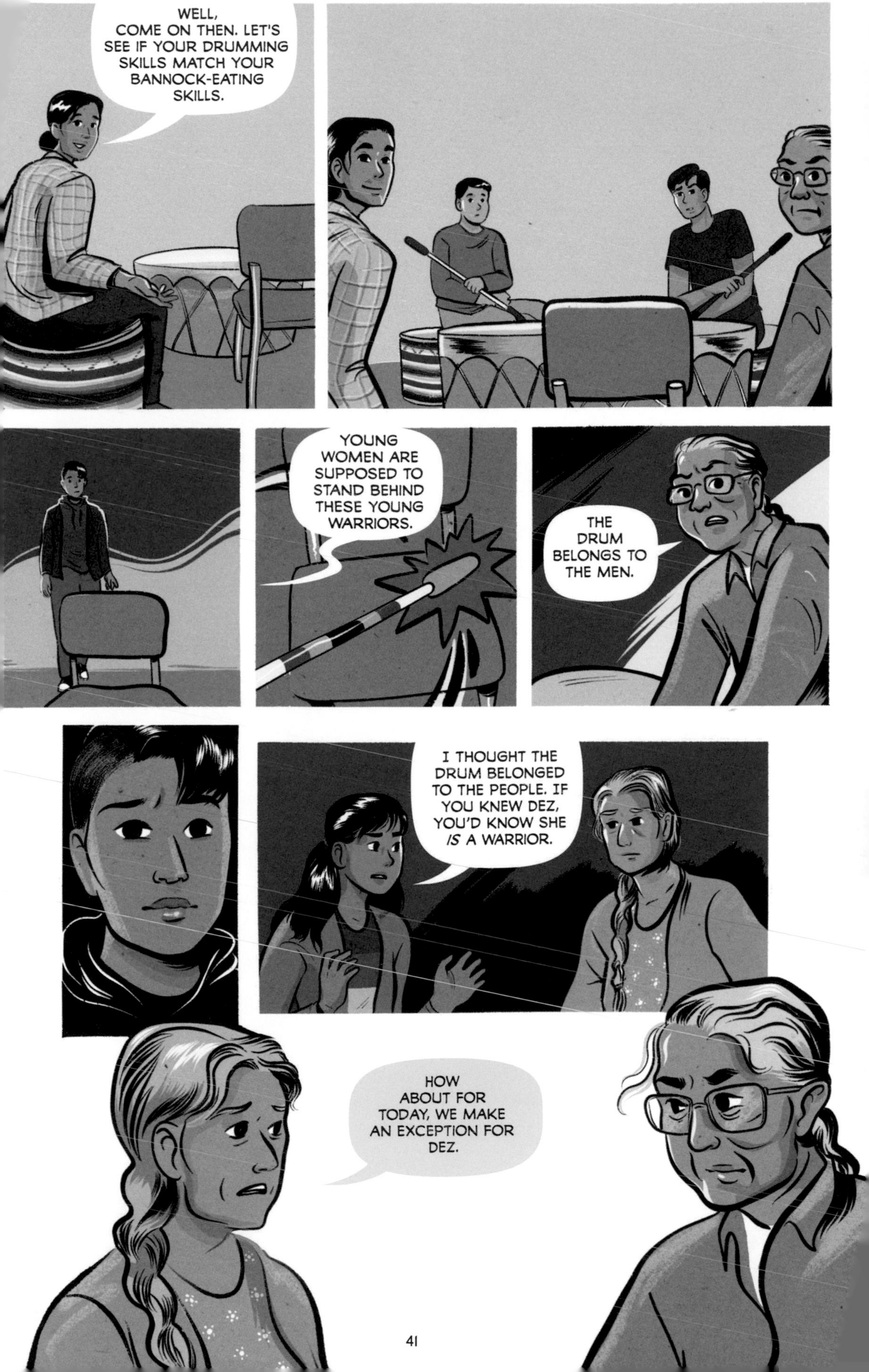
WELL, COME ON THEN. LET'S SEE IF YOUR DRUMMING SKILLS MATCH YOUR BANNOCK-EATING SKILLS.
YOUNG WOMEN ARE SUPPOSED TO STAND BEHIND THESE YOUNG WARRIORS.
THE DRUM BELONGS TO THE MEN.
I THOUGHT THE DRUM BELONGED TO THE PEOPLE. IF YOU KNEW DEZ, YOU'D KNOW SHE *IS* A WARRIOR.
HOW ABOUT FOR TODAY, WE MAKE AN EXCEPTION FOR DEZ.

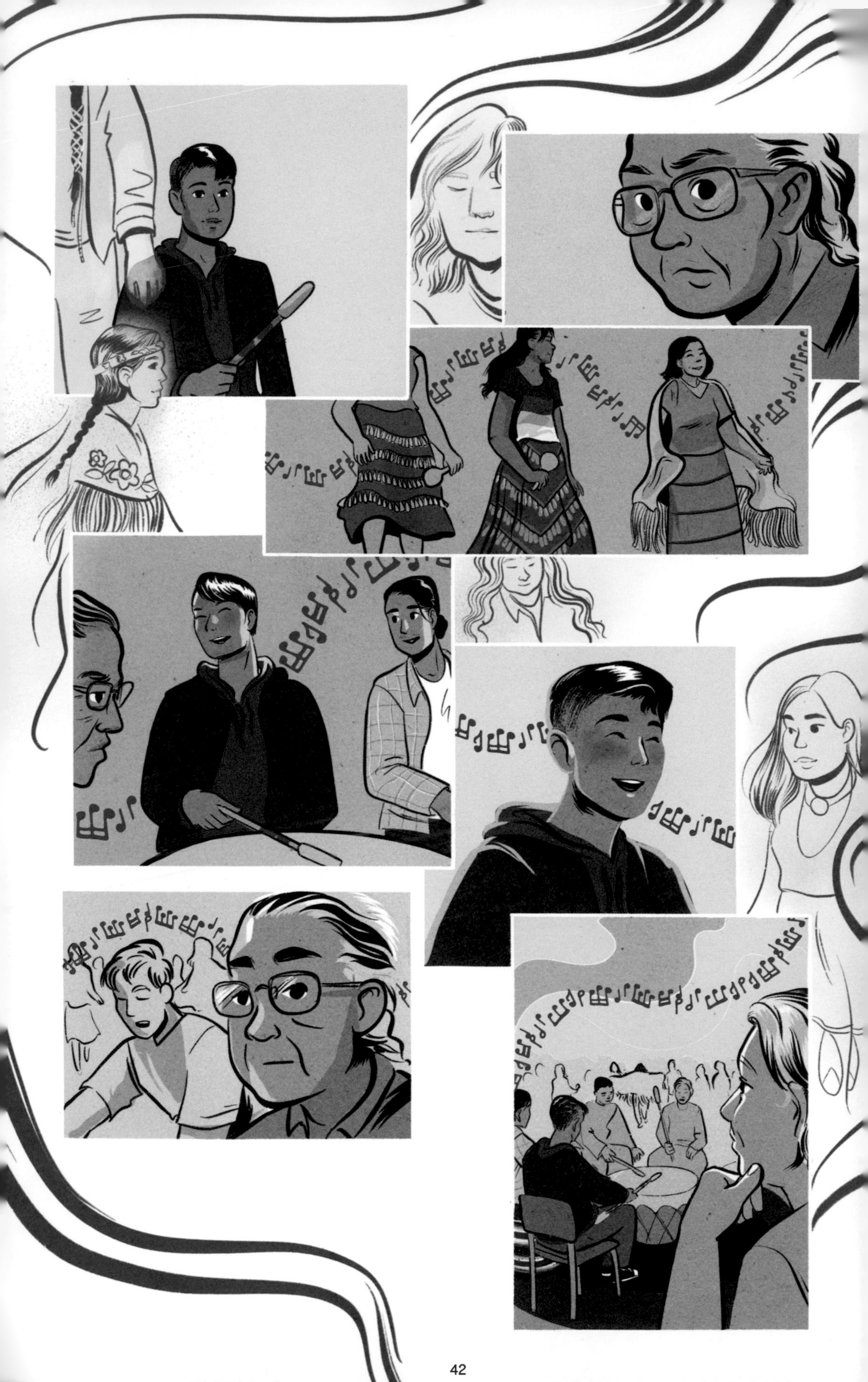

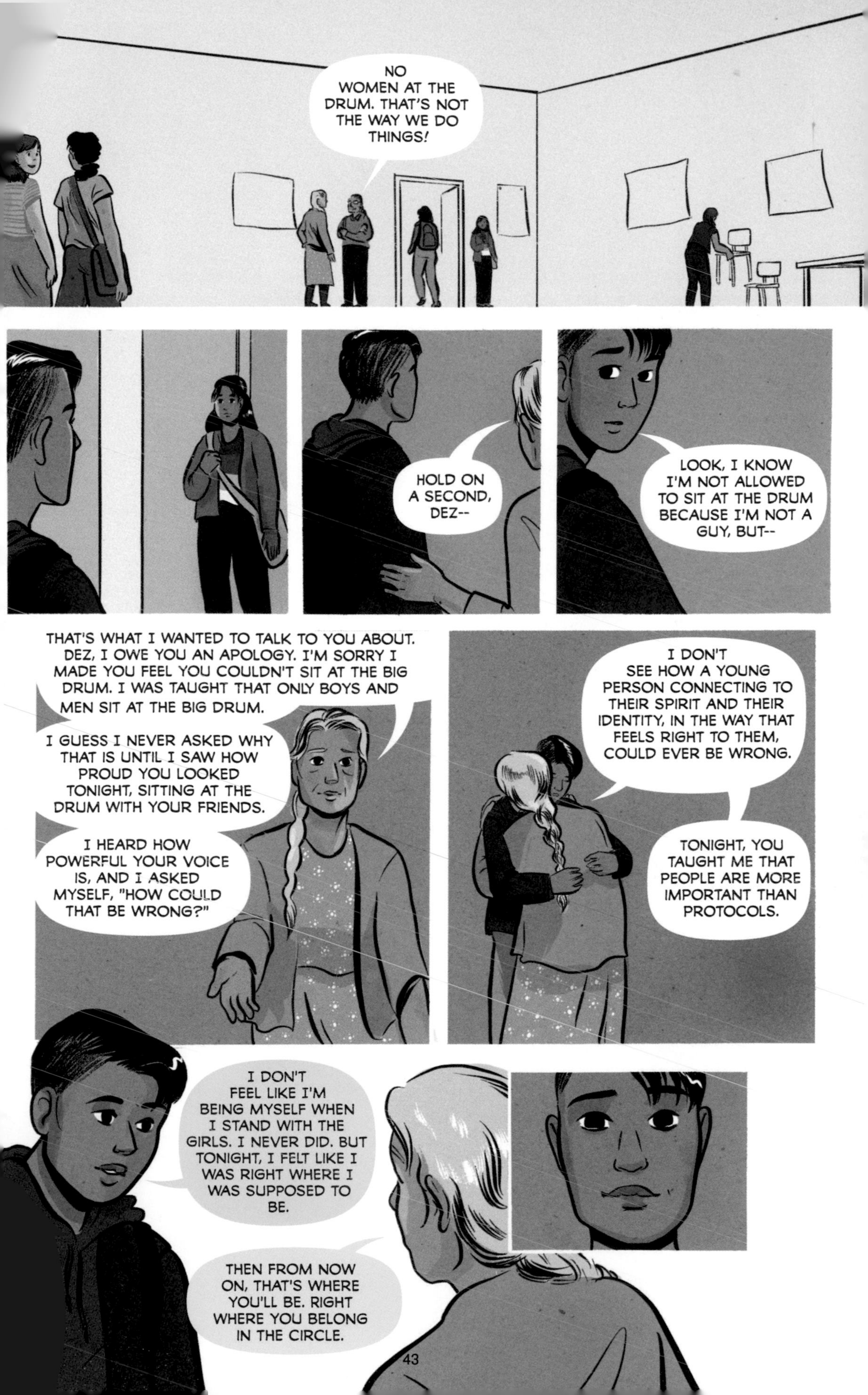
NO WOMEN AT THE DRUM. THAT'S NOT THE WAY WE DO THINGS!
HOLD ON A SECOND, DEZ--
LOOK, I KNOW I'M NOT ALLOWED TO SIT AT THE DRUM BECAUSE I'M NOT A GUY, BUT--
THAT'S WHAT I WANTED TO TALK TO YOU ABOUT. DEZ, I OWE YOU AN APOLOGY. I'M SORRY I MADE YOU FEEL YOU COULDN'T SIT AT THE BIG DRUM. I WAS TAUGHT THAT ONLY BOYS AND MEN SIT AT THE BIG DRUM.
I GUESS I NEVER ASKED WHY THAT IS UNTIL I SAW HOW PROUD YOU LOOKED TONIGHT, SITTING AT THE DRUM WITH YOUR FRIENDS.
I HEARD HOW POWERFUL YOUR VOICE IS, AND I ASKED MYSELF, "HOW COULD THAT BE WRONG?"
I DON'T SEE HOW A YOUNG PERSON CONNECTING TO THEIR SPIRIT AND THEIR IDENTITY, IN THE WAY THAT FEELS RIGHT TO THEM, COULD EVER BE WRONG.
TONIGHT, YOU TAUGHT ME THAT PEOPLE ARE MORE IMPORTANT THAN PROTOCOLS.
I DON'T FEEL LIKE I'M BEING MYSELF WHEN I STAND WITH THE GIRLS. I NEVER DID. BUT TONIGHT, I FELT LIKE I WAS RIGHT WHERE I WAS SUPPOSED TO BE.
THEN FROM NOW ON, THAT'S WHERE YOU'LL BE. RIGHT WHERE YOU BELONG IN THE CIRCLE.

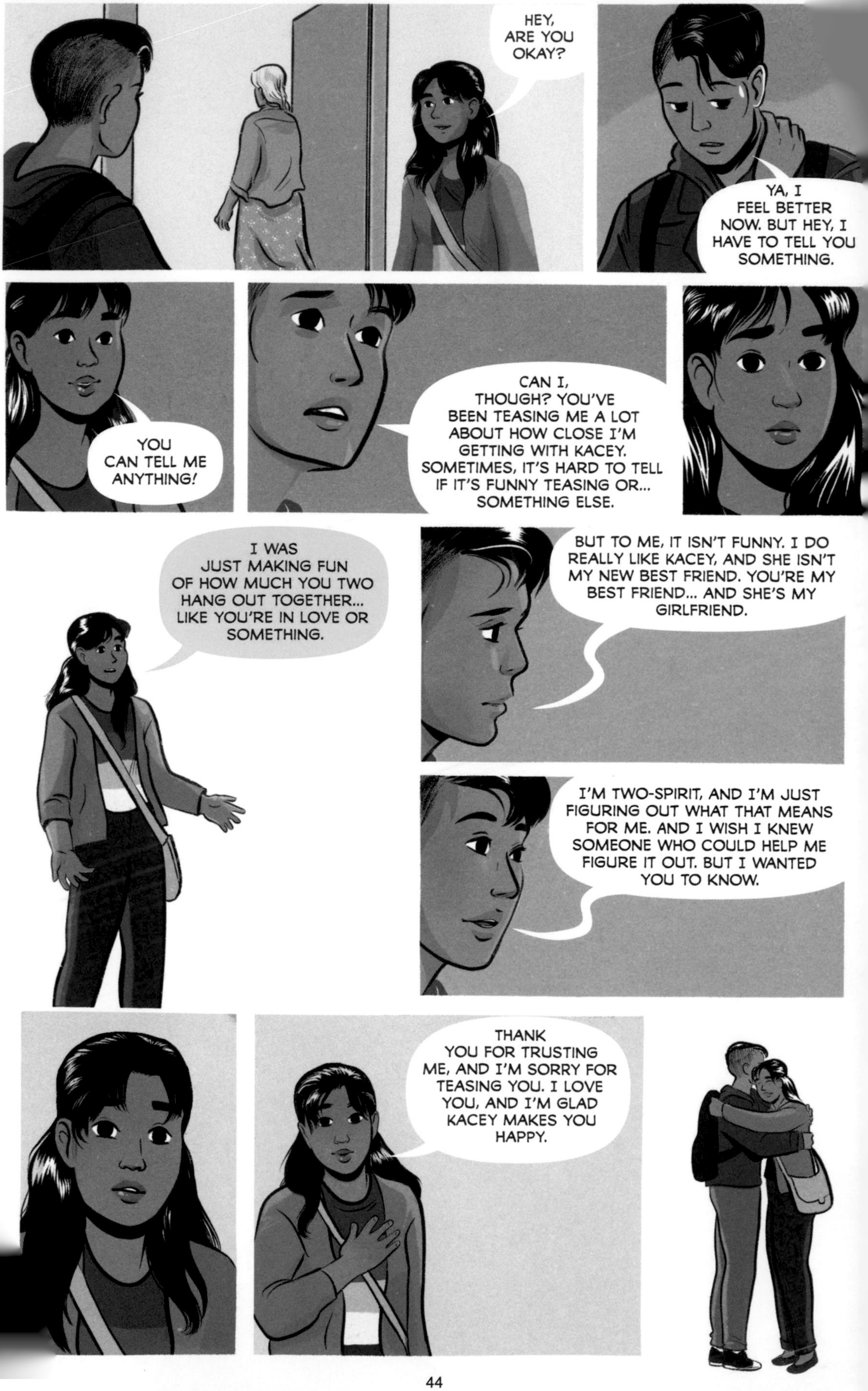

HEY, ARE YOU OKAY?
YA, I FEEL BETTER NOW. BUT HEY, I HAVE TO TELL YOU SOMETHING.
YOU CAN TELL ME ANYTHING!
CAN I, THOUGH? YOU'VE BEEN TEASING ME A LOT ABOUT HOW CLOSE I'M GETTING WITH KACEY. SOMETIMES, IT'S HARD TO TELL IF IT'S FUNNY TEASING OR... SOMETHING ELSE.
I WAS JUST MAKING FUN OF HOW MUCH YOU TWO HANG OUT TOGETHER... LIKE YOU'RE IN LOVE OR SOMETHING.
BUT TO ME, IT ISN'T FUNNY. I DO REALLY LIKE KACEY, AND SHE ISN'T MY NEW BEST FRIEND. YOU'RE MY BEST FRIEND... AND SHE'S MY GIRLFRIEND.
I'M TWO-SPIRIT, AND I'M JUST FIGURING OUT WHAT THAT MEANS FOR ME. AND I WISH I KNEW SOMEONE WHO COULD HELP ME FIGURE IT OUT. BUT I WANTED YOU TO KNOW.
THANK YOU FOR TRUSTING ME, AND I'M SORRY FOR TEASING YOU. I LOVE YOU, AND I'M GLAD KACEY MAKES YOU HAPPY.

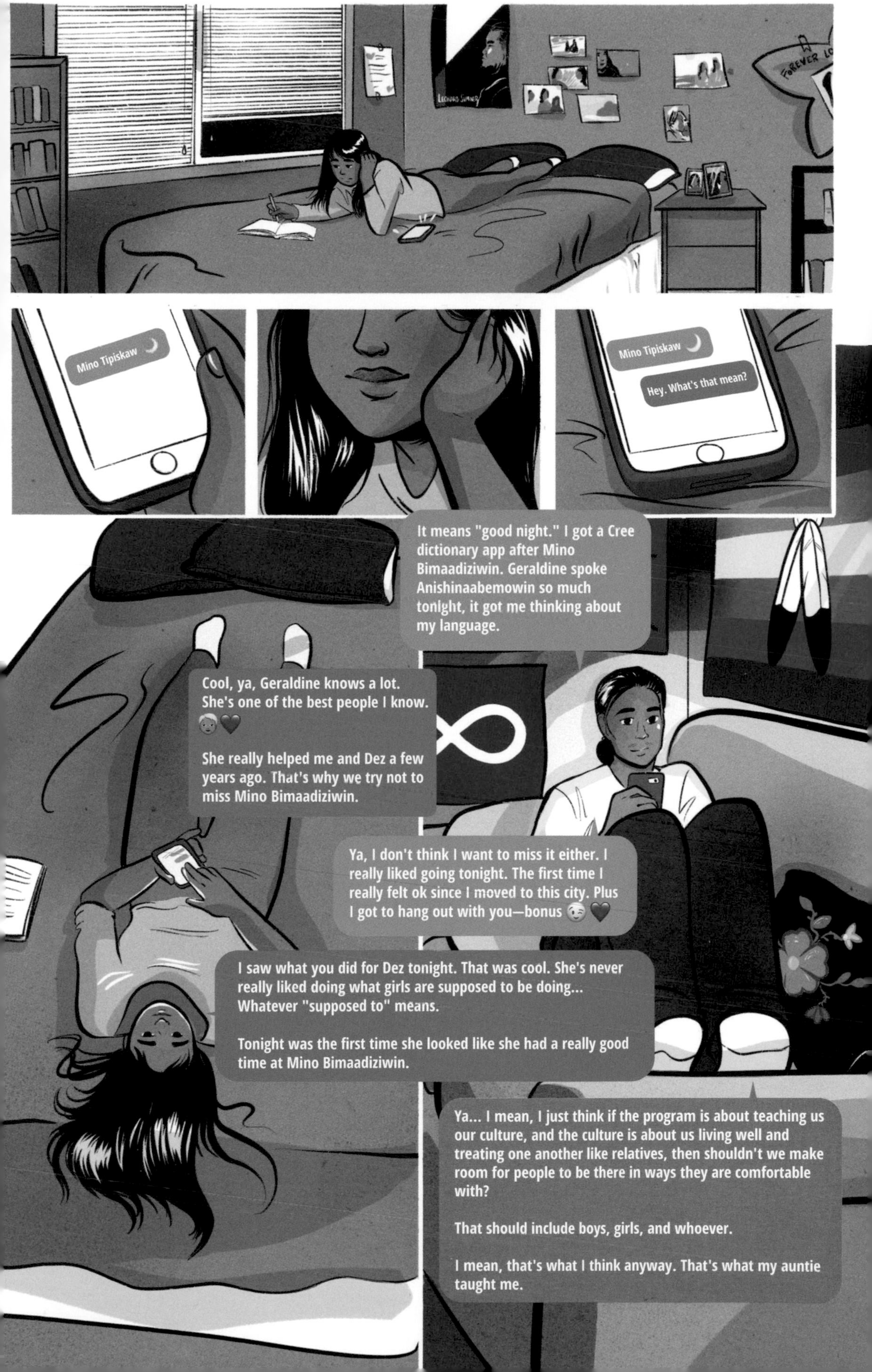
LEONARD SUMNER
FOREVER LO
Mino Tipiskaw
Mino Tipiskaw
Hey. What's that mean?
It means "good night." I got a Cree dictionary app after Mino Bimaadiziwin. Geraldine spoke Anishinaabemowin so much tonight, it got me thinking about my language.
Cool, ya, Geraldine knows a lot. She's one of the best people I know.
She really helped me and Dez a few years ago. That's why we try not to miss Mino Bimaadiziwin.
Ya, I don't think I want to miss it either. I really liked going tonight. The first time I really felt ok since I moved to this city. Plus I got to hang out with you—bonus
I saw what you did for Dez tonight. That was cool. She's never really liked doing what girls are supposed to be doing... Whatever "supposed to" means.
Tonight was the first time she looked like she had a really good time at Mino Bimaadiziwin.
Ya... I mean, I just think if the program is about teaching us our culture, and the culture is about us living well and treating one another like relatives, then shouldn't we make room for people to be there in ways they are comfortable with?
That should include boys, girls, and whoever.
I mean, that's what I think anyway. That's what my auntie taught me.

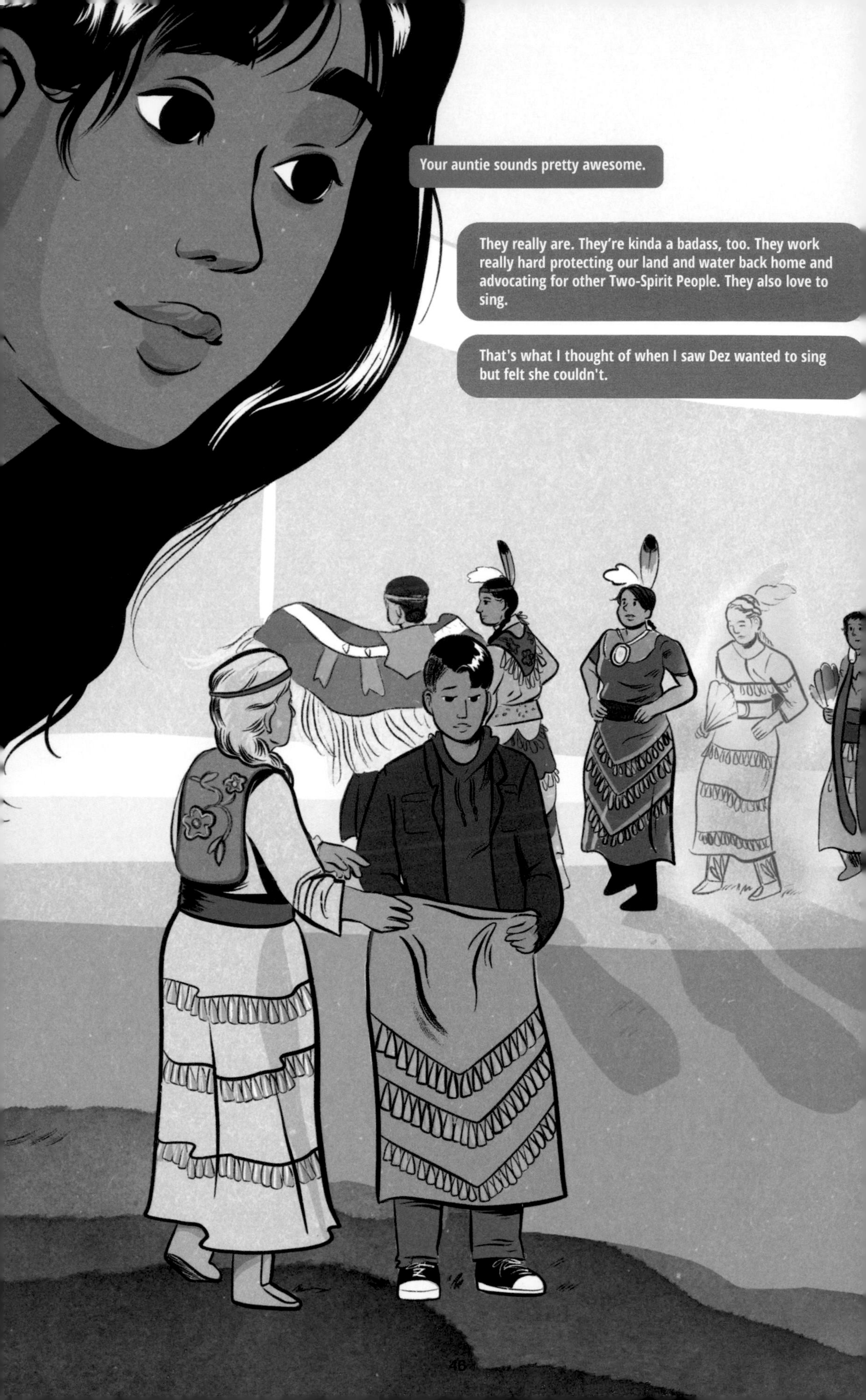
Your auntie sounds pretty awesome.
They really are. They're kinda a badass, too. They work really hard protecting our land and water back home and advocating for other Two-Spirit People. They also love to sing.
That's what I thought of when I saw Dez wanted to sing but felt she couldn't.

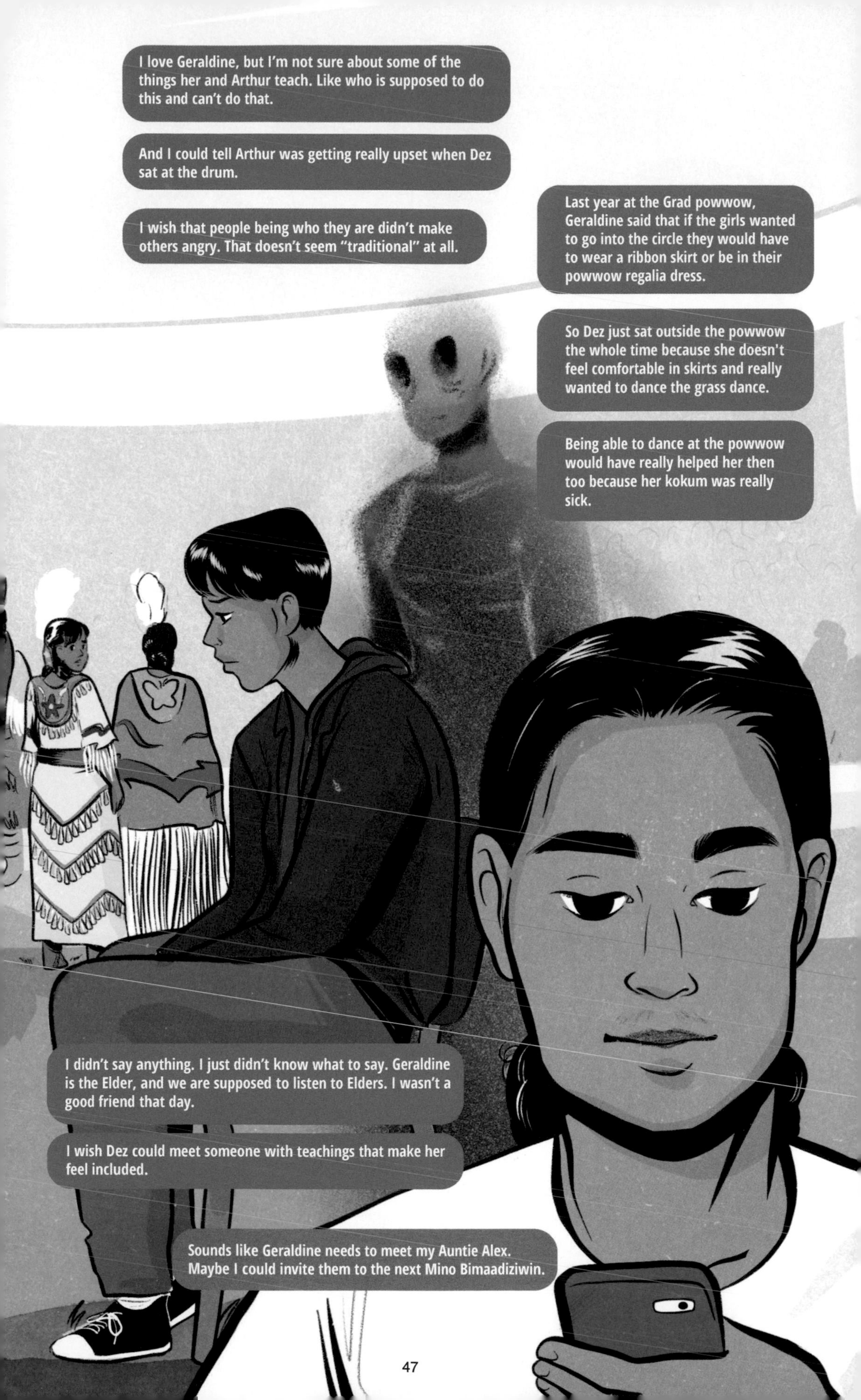
I love Geraldine, but I'm not sure about some of the things her and Arthur teach. Like who is supposed to do this and can't do that.
And I could tell Arthur was getting really upset when Dez sat at the drum.
I wish that people being who they are didn't make others angry. That doesn't seem "traditional" at all.
Last year at the Grad powwow, Geraldine said that if the girls wanted to go into the circle they would have to wear a ribbon skirt or be in their powwow regalia dress.
So Dez just sat outside the powwow the whole time because she doesn't feel comfortable in skirts and really wanted to dance the grass dance.
Being able to dance at the powwow would have really helped her then too because her kokum was really sick.
I didn't say anything. I just didn't know what to say. Geraldine is the Elder, and we are supposed to listen to Elders. I wasn't a good friend that day.
I wish Dez could meet someone with teachings that make her feel included.
Sounds like Geraldine needs to meet my Auntie Alex. Maybe I could invite them to the next Mino Bimaadiziwin.

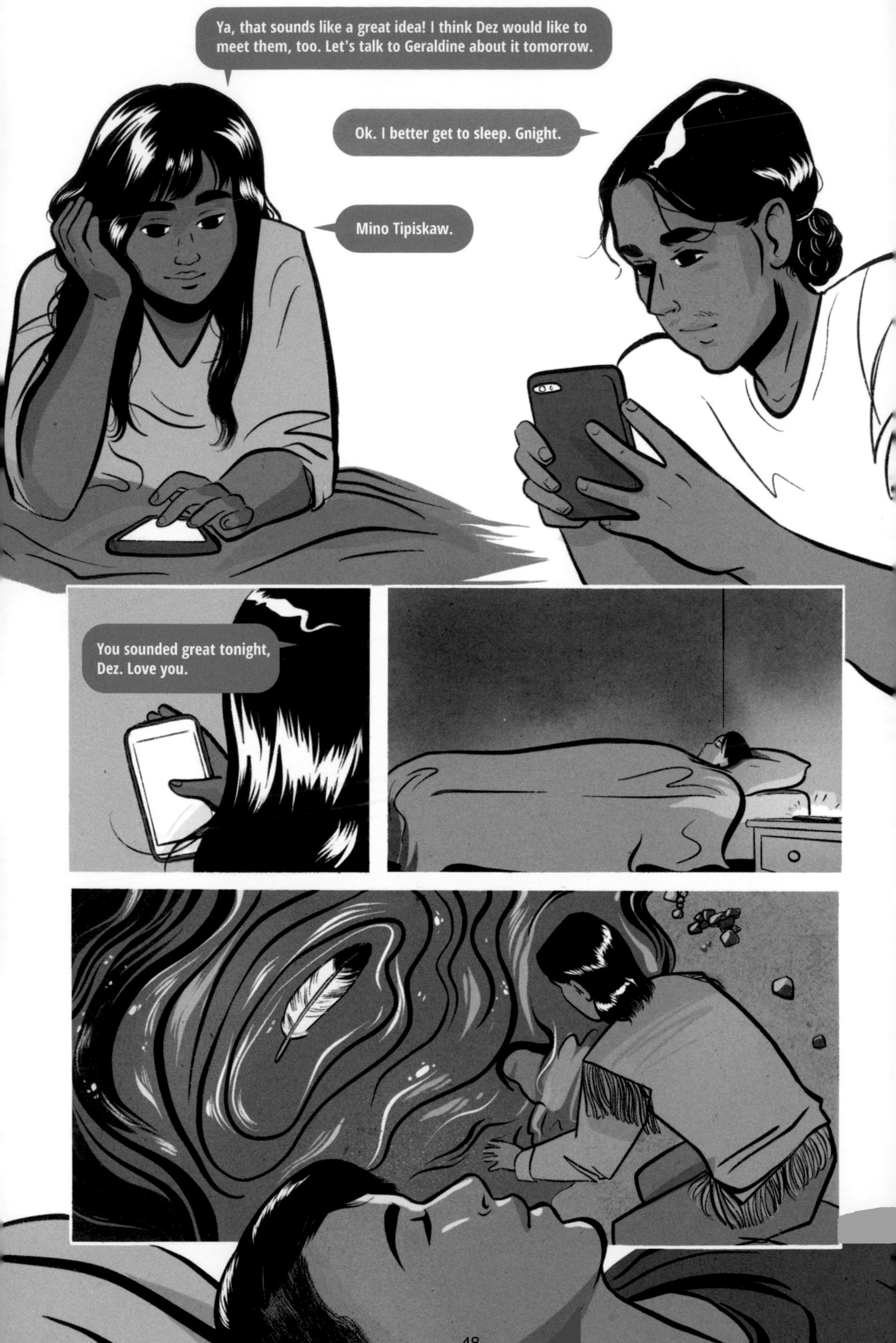
Ya, that sounds like a great idea! I think Dez would like to meet them, too. Let's talk to Geraldine about it tomorrow.
Ok. I better get to sleep. Gnight.
Mino Tipiskaw.
You sounded great tonight, Dez. Love you.

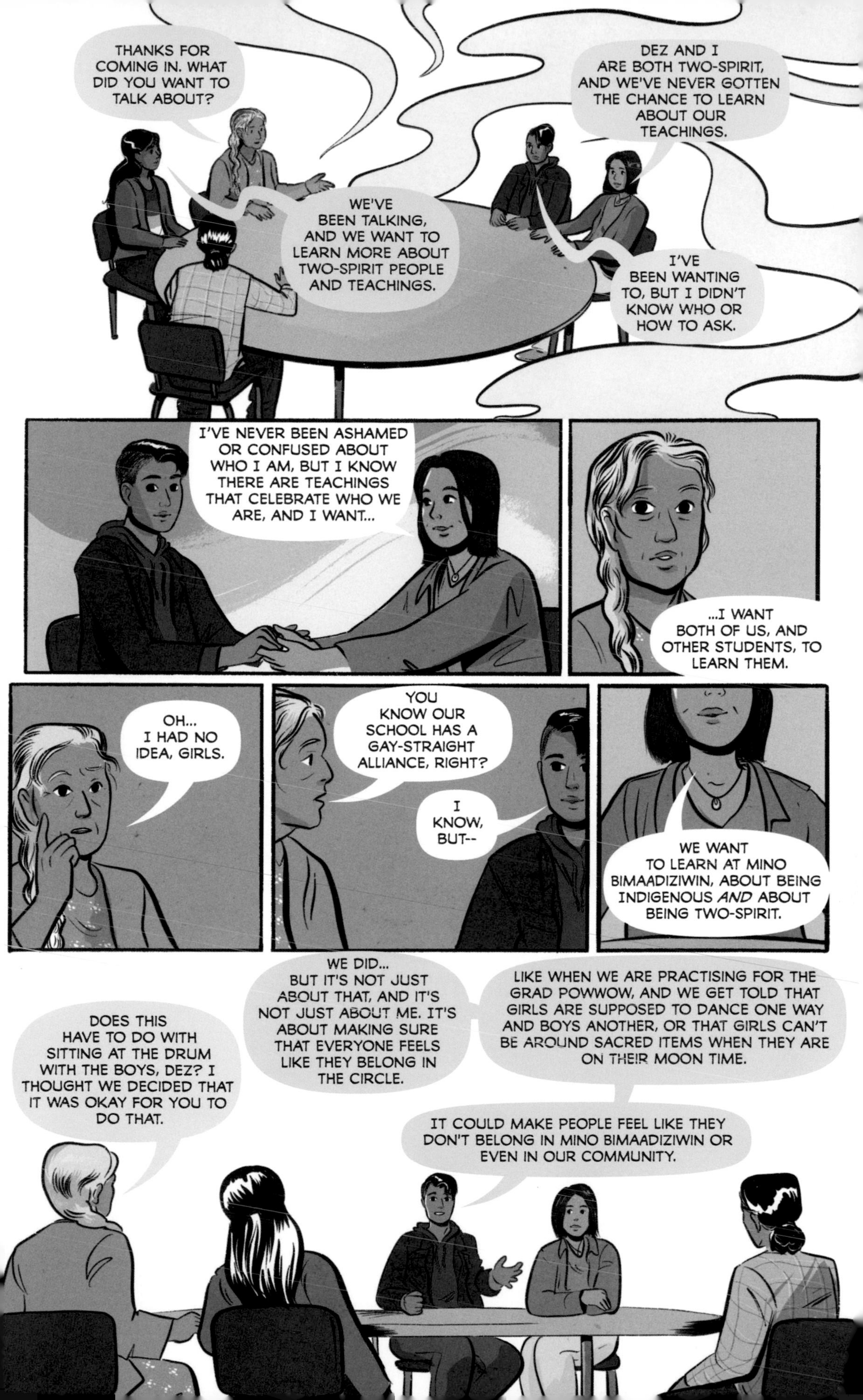
THANKS FOR COMING IN. WHAT DID YOU WANT TO TALK ABOUT?
WE'VE BEEN TALKING, AND WE WANT TO LEARN MORE ABOUT TWO-SPIRIT PEOPLE AND TEACHINGS.
DEZ AND I ARE BOTH TWO-SPIRIT, AND WE'VE NEVER GOTTEN THE CHANCE TO LEARN ABOUT OUR TEACHINGS.
I'VE BEEN WANTING TO, BUT I DIDN'T KNOW WHO OR HOW TO ASK.
I'VE NEVER BEEN ASHAMED OR CONFUSED ABOUT WHO I AM, BUT I KNOW THERE ARE TEACHINGS THAT CELEBRATE WHO WE ARE, AND I WANT...
...I WANT BOTH OF US, AND OTHER STUDENTS, TO LEARN THEM.
OH... I HAD NO IDEA, GIRLS.
YOU KNOW OUR SCHOOL HAS A GAY-STRAIGHT ALLIANCE, RIGHT?
I KNOW, BUT--
WE WANT TO LEARN AT MINO BIMAADIZIWIN, ABOUT BEING INDIGENOUS *AND* ABOUT BEING TWO-SPIRIT.
DOES THIS HAVE TO DO WITH SITTING AT THE DRUM WITH THE BOYS, DEZ? I THOUGHT WE DECIDED THAT IT WAS OKAY FOR YOU TO DO THAT.
WE DID... BUT IT'S NOT JUST ABOUT THAT, AND IT'S NOT JUST ABOUT ME. IT'S ABOUT MAKING SURE THAT EVERYONE FEELS LIKE THEY BELONG IN THE CIRCLE.
LIKE WHEN WE ARE PRACTISING FOR THE GRAD POWWOW, AND WE GET TOLD THAT GIRLS ARE SUPPOSED TO DANCE ONE WAY AND BOYS ANOTHER, OR THAT GIRLS CAN'T BE AROUND SACRED ITEMS WHEN THEY ARE ON THEIR MOON TIME.
IT COULD MAKE PEOPLE FEEL LIKE THEY DON'T BELONG IN MINO BIMAADIZIWIN OR EVEN IN OUR COMMUNITY.

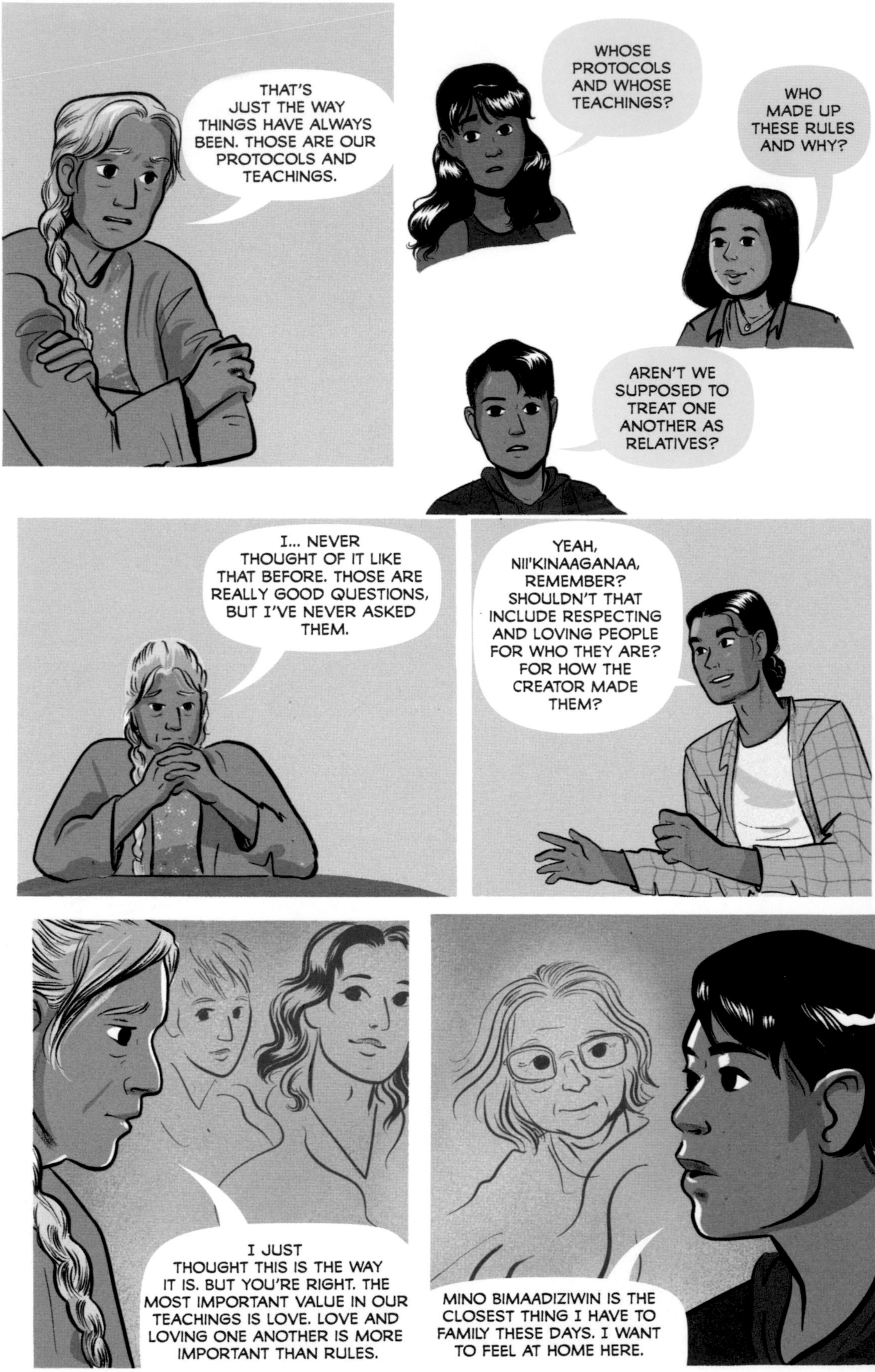
THAT'S JUST THE WAY THINGS HAVE ALWAYS BEEN. THOSE ARE OUR PROTOCOLS AND TEACHINGS.
WHOSE PROTOCOLS AND WHOSE TEACHINGS?
WHO MADE UP THESE RULES AND WHY?
AREN'T WE SUPPOSED TO TREAT ONE ANOTHER AS RELATIVES?
I... NEVER THOUGHT OF IT LIKE THAT BEFORE. THOSE ARE REALLY GOOD QUESTIONS, BUT I'VE NEVER ASKED THEM.
YEAH, NII'KINAAGANAA, REMEMBER? SHOULDN'T THAT INCLUDE RESPECTING AND LOVING PEOPLE FOR WHO THEY ARE? FOR HOW THE CREATOR MADE THEM?
I JUST THOUGHT THIS IS THE WAY IT IS. BUT YOU'RE RIGHT. THE MOST IMPORTANT VALUE IN OUR TEACHINGS IS LOVE. LOVE AND LOVING ONE ANOTHER IS MORE IMPORTANT THAN RULES.
MINO BIMAADIZIWIN IS THE CLOSEST THING I HAVE TO FAMILY THESE DAYS. I WANT TO FEEL AT HOME HERE.

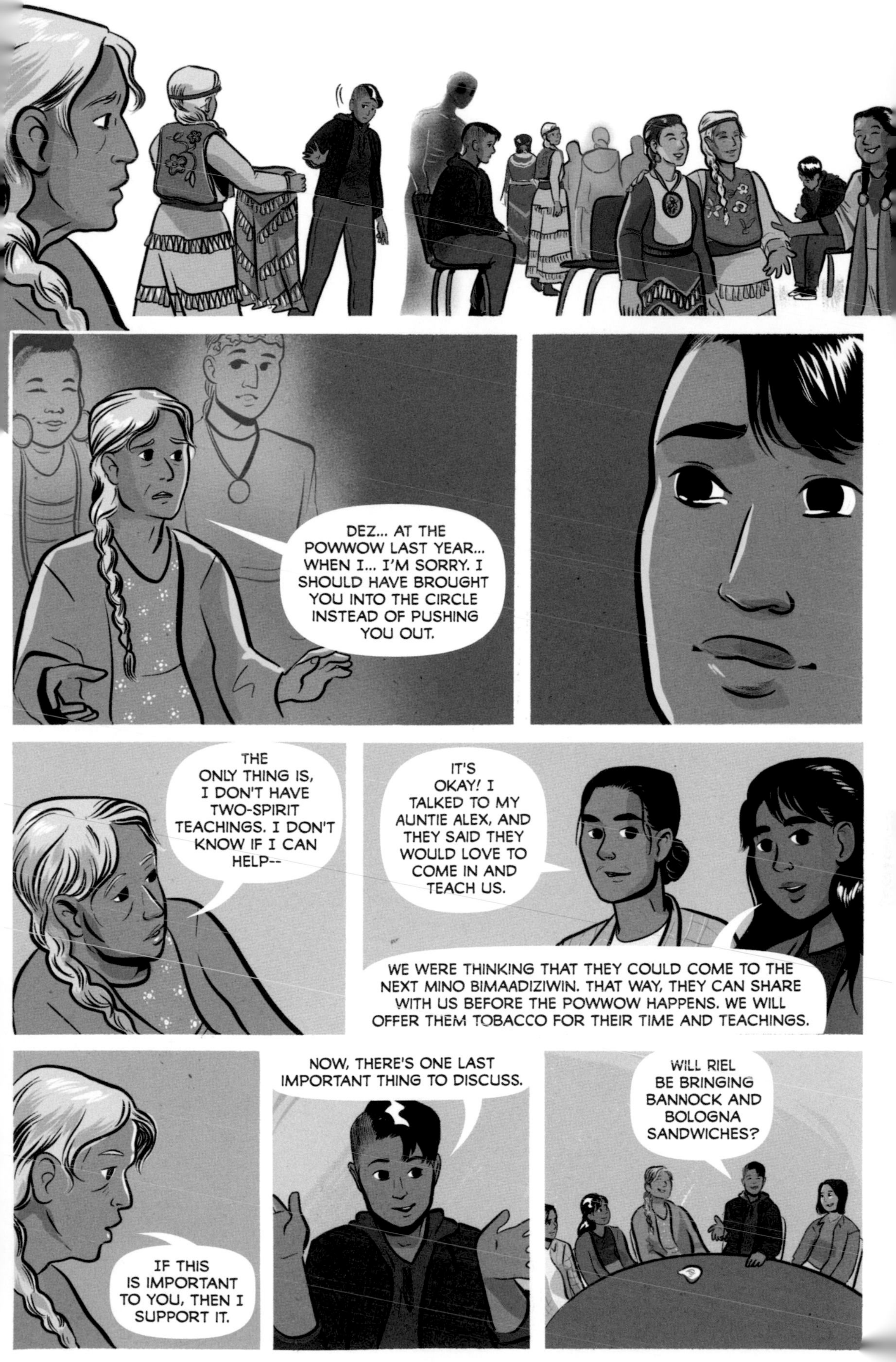
DEZ... AT THE POWWOW LAST YEAR... WHEN I... I'M SORRY. I SHOULD HAVE BROUGHT YOU INTO THE CIRCLE INSTEAD OF PUSHING YOU OUT.
THE ONLY THING IS, I DON'T HAVE TWO-SPIRIT TEACHINGS. I DON'T KNOW IF I CAN HELP--
IT'S OKAY! I TALKED TO MY AUNTIE ALEX, AND THEY SAID THEY WOULD LOVE TO COME IN AND TEACH US.
WE WERE THINKING THAT THEY COULD COME TO THE NEXT MINO BIMAADIZIWIN. THAT WAY, THEY CAN SHARE WITH US BEFORE THE POWWOW HAPPENS. WE WILL OFFER THEM TOBACCO FOR THEIR TIME AND TEACHINGS.
IF THIS IS IMPORTANT TO YOU, THEN I SUPPORT IT.
NOW, THERE'S ONE LAST IMPORTANT THING TO DISCUSS.
WILL RIEL BE BRINGING BANNOCK AND BOLOGNA SANDWICHES?

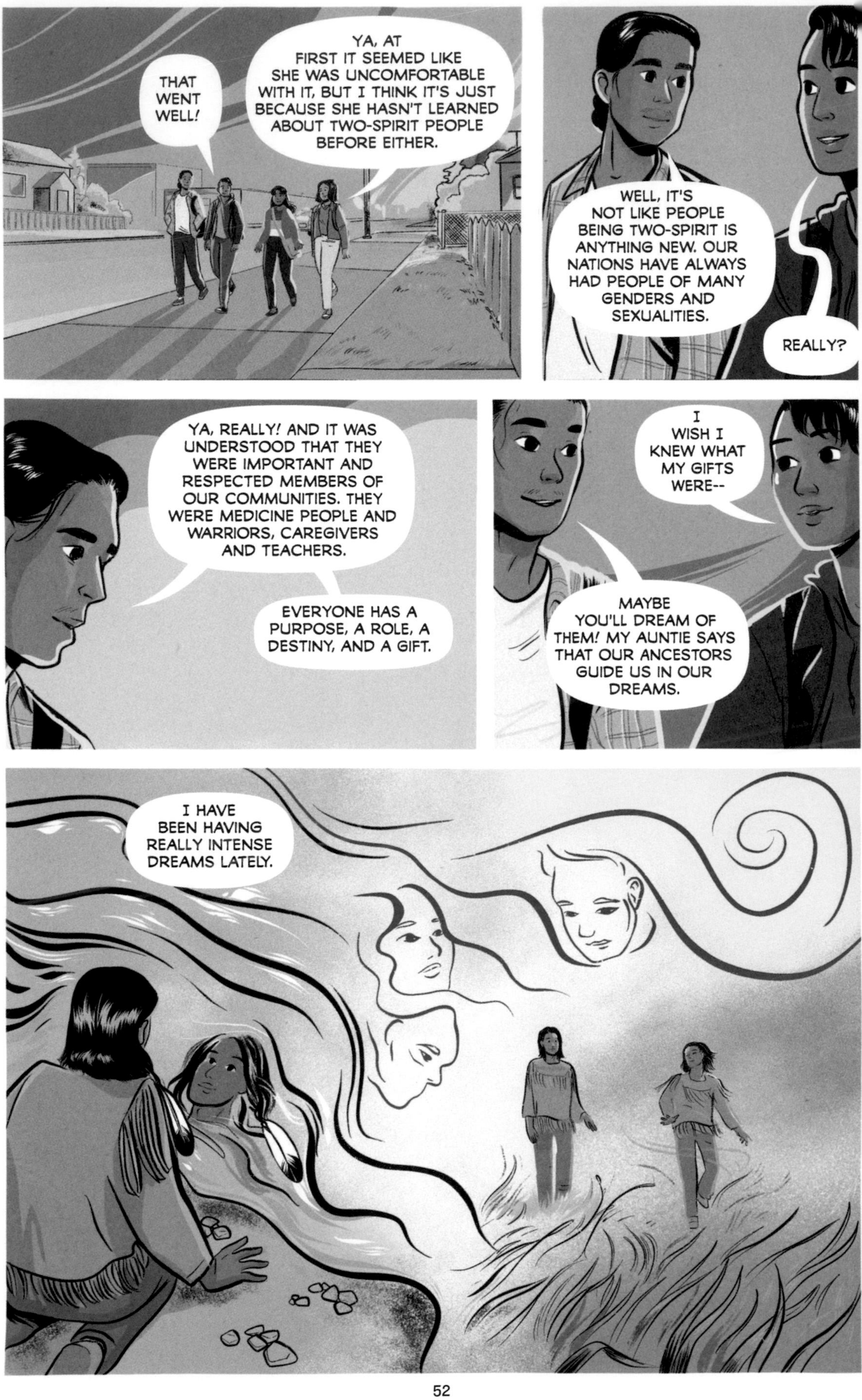
THAT WENT WELL!
YA, AT FIRST IT SEEMED LIKE SHE WAS UNCOMFORTABLE WITH IT, BUT I THINK IT'S JUST BECAUSE SHE HASN'T LEARNED ABOUT TWO-SPIRIT PEOPLE BEFORE EITHER.
WELL, IT'S NOT LIKE PEOPLE BEING TWO-SPIRIT IS ANYTHING NEW. OUR NATIONS HAVE ALWAYS HAD PEOPLE OF MANY GENDERS AND SEXUALITIES.
REALLY?
YA, REALLY! AND IT WAS UNDERSTOOD THAT THEY WERE IMPORTANT AND RESPECTED MEMBERS OF OUR COMMUNITIES. THEY WERE MEDICINE PEOPLE AND WARRIORS, CAREGIVERS AND TEACHERS.
EVERYONE HAS A PURPOSE, A ROLE, A DESTINY, AND A GIFT.
I WISH I KNEW WHAT MY GIFTS WERE--
MAYBE YOU'LL DREAM OF THEM! MY AUNTIE SAYS THAT OUR ANCESTORS GUIDE US IN OUR DREAMS.
I HAVE BEEN HAVING REALLY INTENSE DREAMS LATELY.

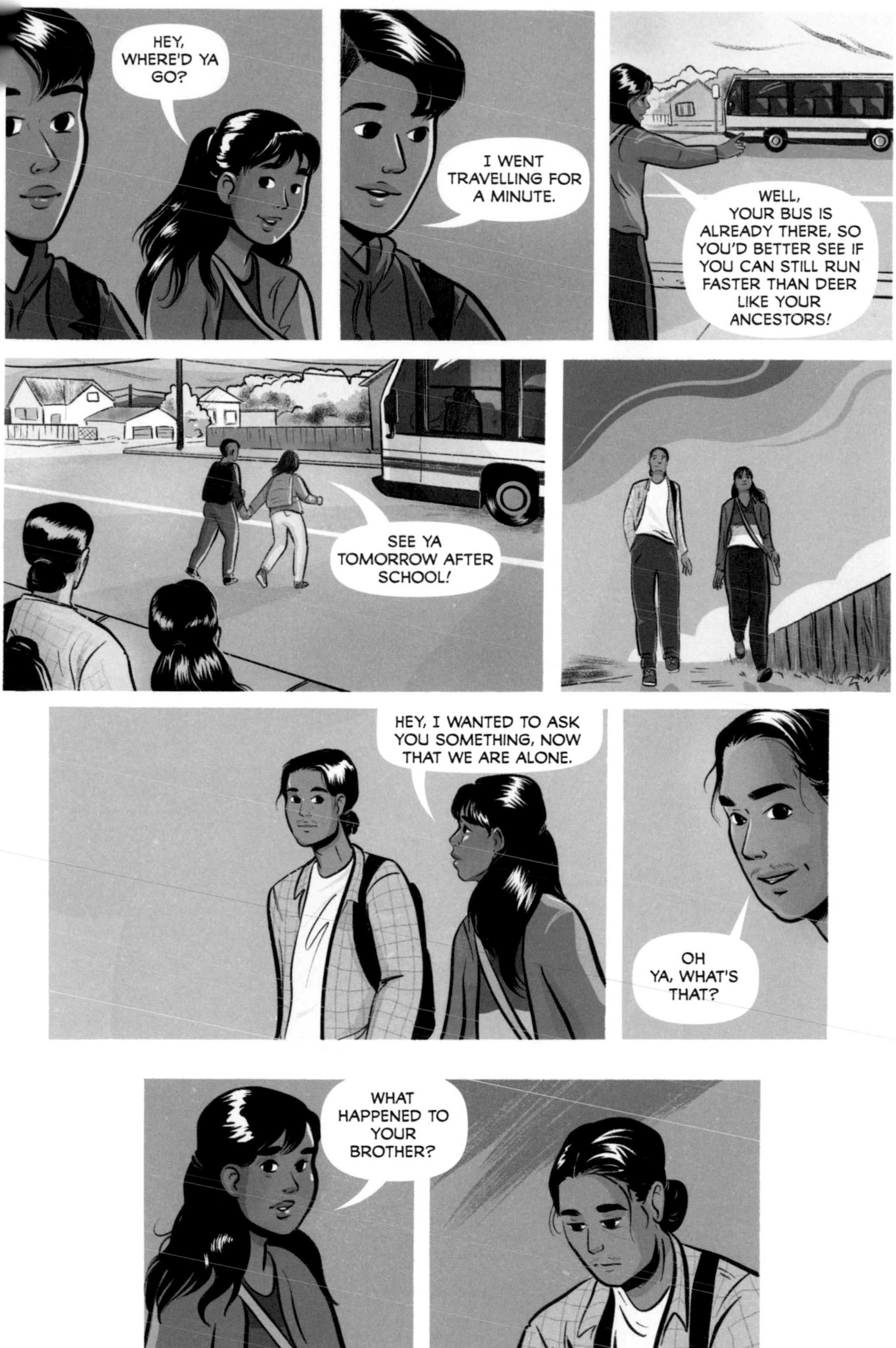
HEY, WHERE'D YA GO?
I WENT TRAVELLING FOR A MINUTE.
WELL, YOUR BUS IS ALREADY THERE, SO YOU'D BETTER SEE IF YOU CAN STILL RUN FASTER THAN DEER LIKE YOUR ANCESTORS!
SEE YA TOMORROW AFTER SCHOOL!
HEY, I WANTED TO ASK YOU SOMETHING, NOW THAT WE ARE ALONE.
OH YA, WHAT'S THAT?
WHAT HAPPENED TO YOUR BROTHER?

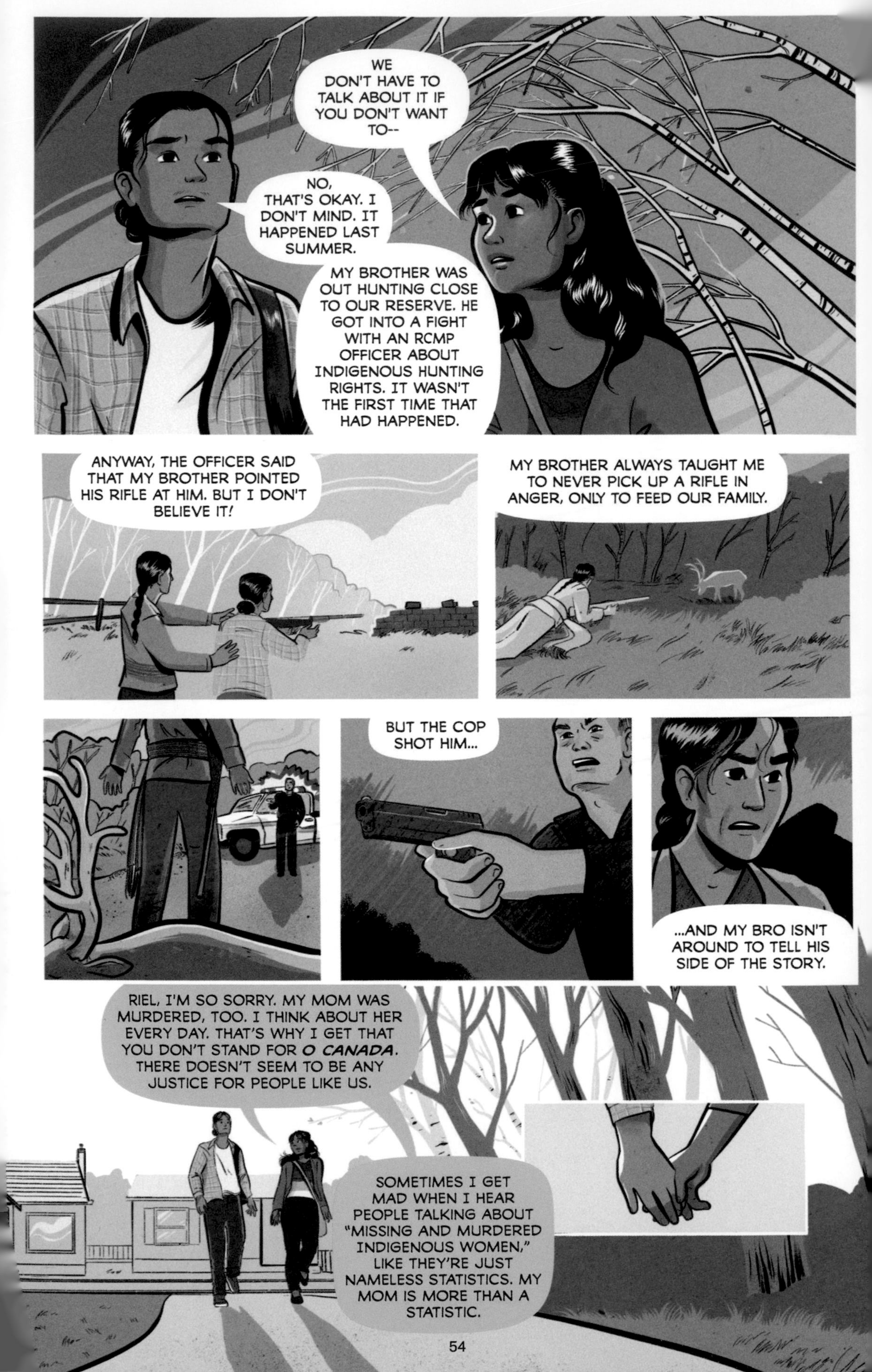
WE DON'T HAVE TO TALK ABOUT IT IF YOU DON'T WANT TO--
NO, THAT'S OKAY. I DON'T MIND. IT HAPPENED LAST SUMMER.
MY BROTHER WAS OUT HUNTING CLOSE TO OUR RESERVE. HE GOT INTO A FIGHT WITH AN RCMP OFFICER ABOUT INDIGENOUS HUNTING RIGHTS. IT WASN'T THE FIRST TIME THAT HAD HAPPENED.
ANYWAY, THE OFFICER SAID THAT MY BROTHER POINTED HIS RIFLE AT HIM. BUT I DON'T BELIEVE IT!
MY BROTHER ALWAYS TAUGHT ME TO NEVER PICK UP A RIFLE IN ANGER, ONLY TO FEED OUR FAMILY.
BUT THE COP SHOT HIM...
...AND MY BRO ISN'T AROUND TO TELL HIS SIDE OF THE STORY.
RIEL, I'M SO SORRY. MY MOM WAS MURDERED, TOO. I THINK ABOUT HER EVERY DAY. THAT'S WHY I GET THAT YOU DON'T STAND FOR *O CANADA*. THERE DOESN'T SEEM TO BE ANY JUSTICE FOR PEOPLE LIKE US.
SOMETIMES I GET MAD WHEN I HEAR PEOPLE TALKING ABOUT "MISSING AND MURDERED INDIGENOUS WOMEN," LIKE THEY'RE JUST NAMELESS STATISTICS. MY MOM IS MORE THAN A STATISTIC.

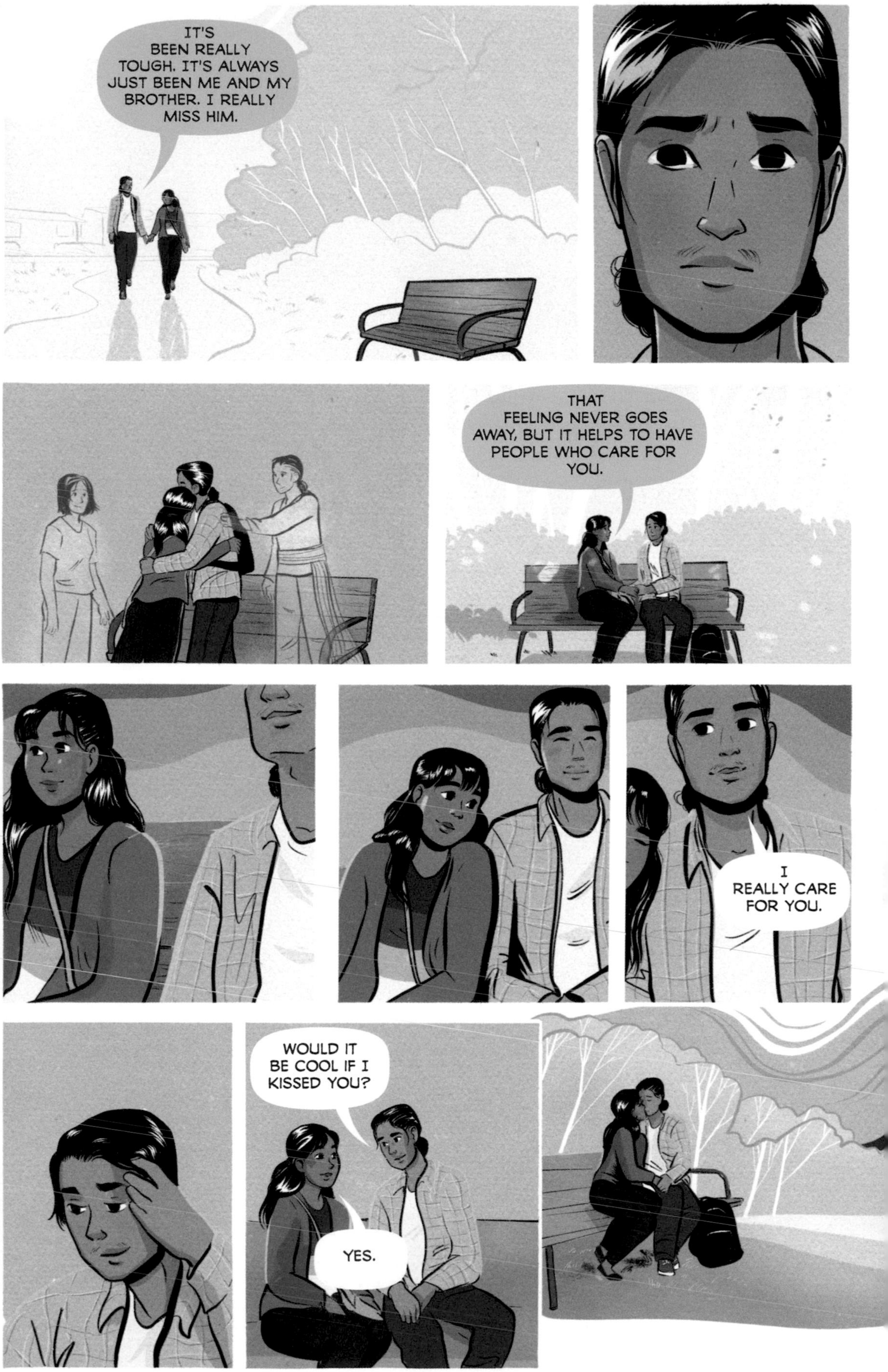
IT'S BEEN REALLY TOUGH. IT'S ALWAYS JUST BEEN ME AND MY BROTHER. I REALLY MISS HIM.
THAT FEELING NEVER GOES AWAY, BUT IT HELPS TO HAVE PEOPLE WHO CARE FOR YOU.
I REALLY CARE FOR YOU.
WOULD IT BE COOL IF I KISSED YOU?
YES.

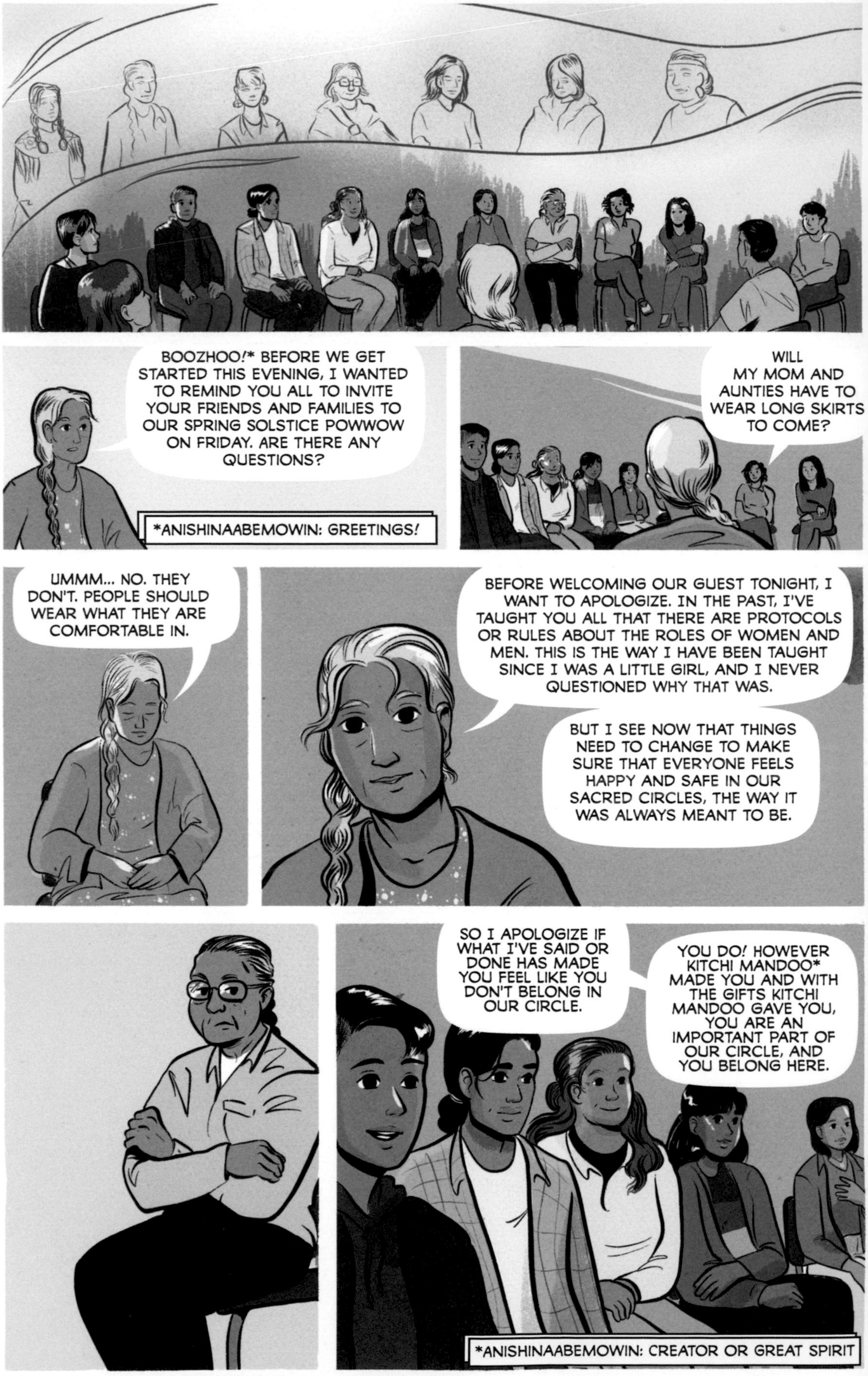
BOOZHOO!* BEFORE WE GET STARTED THIS EVENING, I WANTED TO REMIND YOU ALL TO INVITE YOUR FRIENDS AND FAMILIES TO OUR SPRING SOLSTICE POWWOW ON FRIDAY. ARE THERE ANY QUESTIONS?
*ANISHINAABEMOWIN: GREETINGS!
WILL MY MOM AND AUNTIES HAVE TO WEAR LONG SKIRTS TO COME?
UMMM... NO. THEY DON'T. PEOPLE SHOULD WEAR WHAT THEY ARE COMFORTABLE IN.
BEFORE WELCOMING OUR GUEST TONIGHT, I WANT TO APOLOGIZE. IN THE PAST, I'VE TAUGHT YOU ALL THAT THERE ARE PROTOCOLS OR RULES ABOUT THE ROLES OF WOMEN AND MEN. THIS IS THE WAY I HAVE BEEN TAUGHT SINCE I WAS A LITTLE GIRL, AND I NEVER QUESTIONED WHY THAT WAS.
BUT I SEE NOW THAT THINGS NEED TO CHANGE TO MAKE SURE THAT EVERYONE FEELS HAPPY AND SAFE IN OUR SACRED CIRCLES, THE WAY IT WAS ALWAYS MEANT TO BE.
SO I APOLOGIZE IF WHAT I'VE SAID OR DONE HAS MADE YOU FEEL LIKE YOU DON'T BELONG IN OUR CIRCLE.
YOU DO! HOWEVER KITCHI MANDOO* MADE YOU AND WITH THE GIFTS KITCHI MANDOO GAVE YOU, YOU ARE AN IMPORTANT PART OF OUR CIRCLE, AND YOU BELONG HERE.
*ANISHINAABEMOWIN: CREATOR OR GREAT SPIRIT

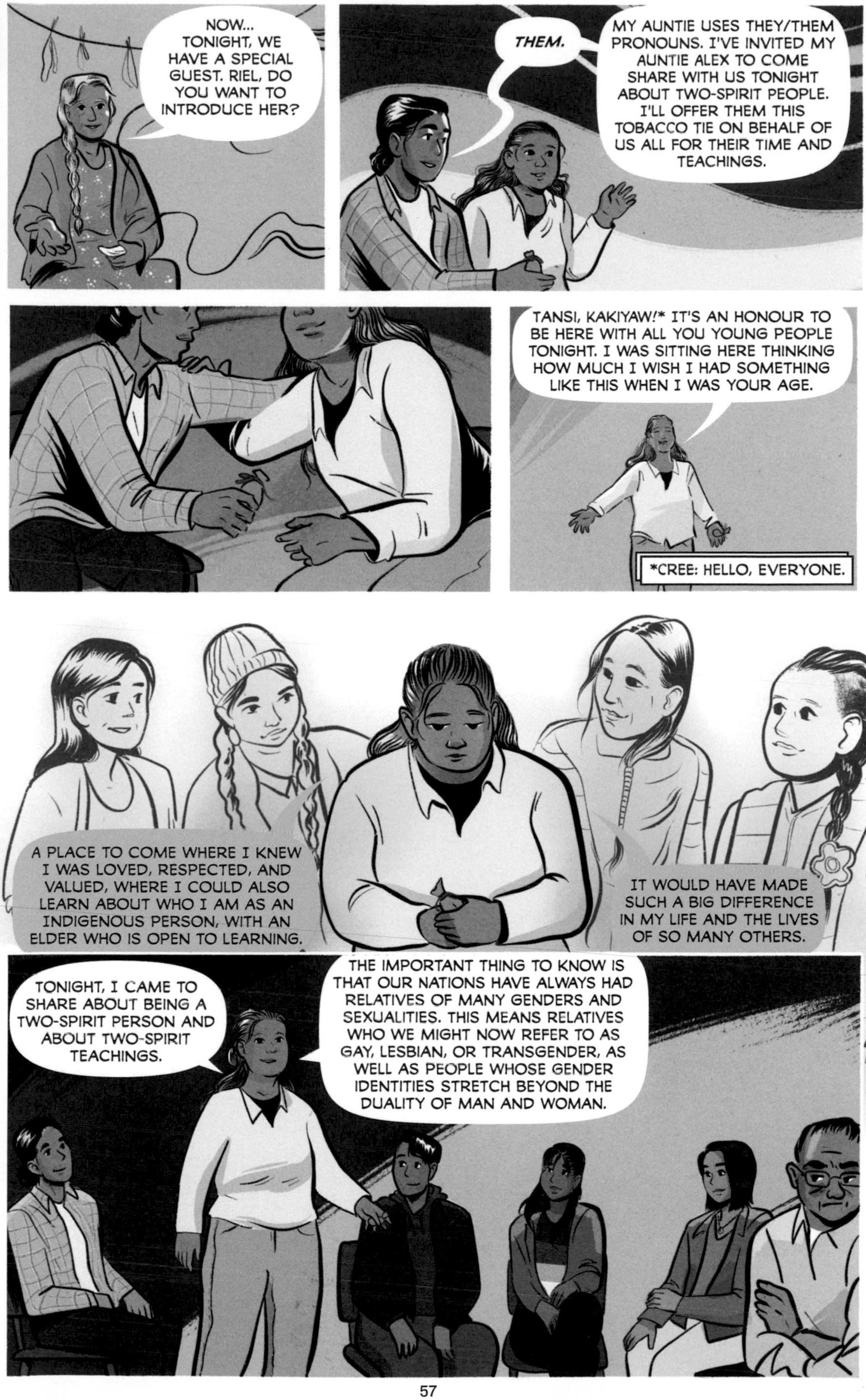
NOW... TONIGHT, WE HAVE A SPECIAL GUEST. RIEL, DO YOU WANT TO INTRODUCE HER?
THEM.
MY AUNTIE USES THEY/THEM PRONOUNS. I'VE INVITED MY AUNTIE ALEX TO COME SHARE WITH US TONIGHT ABOUT TWO-SPIRIT PEOPLE. I'LL OFFER THEM THIS TOBACCO TIE ON BEHALF OF US ALL FOR THEIR TIME AND TEACHINGS.
TANSI, KAKIYAW!* IT'S AN HONOUR TO BE HERE WITH ALL YOU YOUNG PEOPLE TONIGHT. I WAS SITTING HERE THINKING HOW MUCH I WISH I HAD SOMETHING LIKE THIS WHEN I WAS YOUR AGE.
*CREE: HELLO, EVERYONE.
A PLACE TO COME WHERE I KNEW I WAS LOVED, RESPECTED, AND VALUED, WHERE I COULD ALSO LEARN ABOUT WHO I AM AS AN INDIGENOUS PERSON, WITH AN ELDER WHO IS OPEN TO LEARNING.
IT WOULD HAVE MADE SUCH A BIG DIFFERENCE IN MY LIFE AND THE LIVES OF SO MANY OTHERS.
TONIGHT, I CAME TO SHARE ABOUT BEING A TWO-SPIRIT PERSON AND ABOUT TWO-SPIRIT TEACHINGS.
THE IMPORTANT THING TO KNOW IS THAT OUR NATIONS HAVE ALWAYS HAD RELATIVES OF MANY GENDERS AND SEXUALITIES. THIS MEANS RELATIVES WHO WE MIGHT NOW REFER TO AS GAY, LESBIAN, OR TRANSGENDER, AS WELL AS PEOPLE WHOSE GENDER IDENTITIES STRETCH BEYOND THE DUALITY OF MAN AND WOMAN.

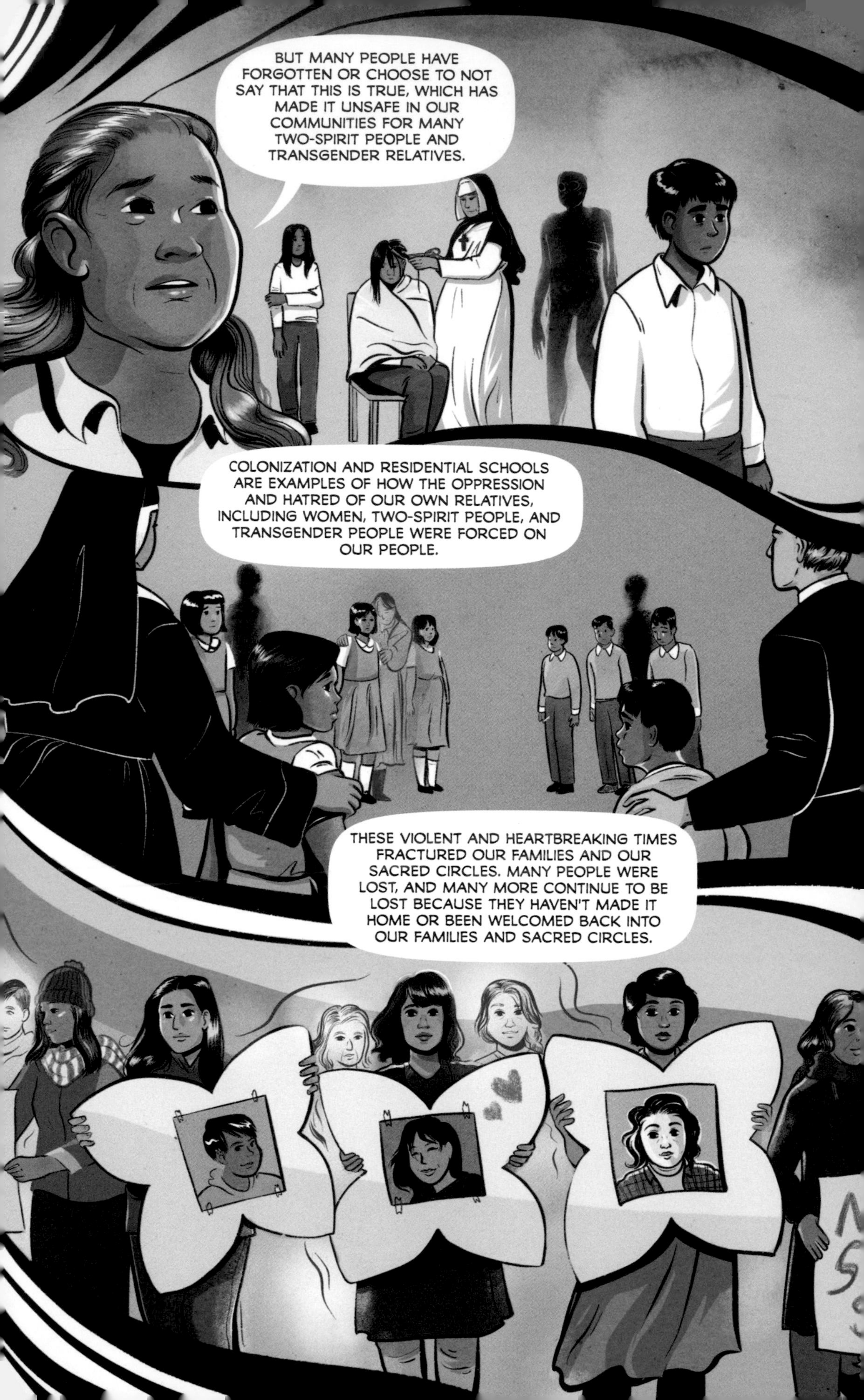
BUT MANY PEOPLE HAVE FORGOTTEN OR CHOOSE TO NOT SAY THAT THIS IS TRUE, WHICH HAS MADE IT UNSAFE IN OUR COMMUNITIES FOR MANY TWO-SPIRIT PEOPLE AND TRANSGENDER RELATIVES.
COLONIZATION AND RESIDENTIAL SCHOOLS ARE EXAMPLES OF HOW THE OPPRESSION AND HATRED OF OUR OWN RELATIVES, INCLUDING WOMEN, TWO-SPIRIT PEOPLE, AND TRANSGENDER PEOPLE WERE FORCED ON OUR PEOPLE.
THESE VIOLENT AND HEARTBREAKING TIMES FRACTURED OUR FAMILIES AND OUR SACRED CIRCLES. MANY PEOPLE WERE LOST, AND MANY MORE CONTINUE TO BE LOST BECAUSE THEY HAVEN'T MADE IT HOME OR BEEN WELCOMED BACK INTO OUR FAMILIES AND SACRED CIRCLES.

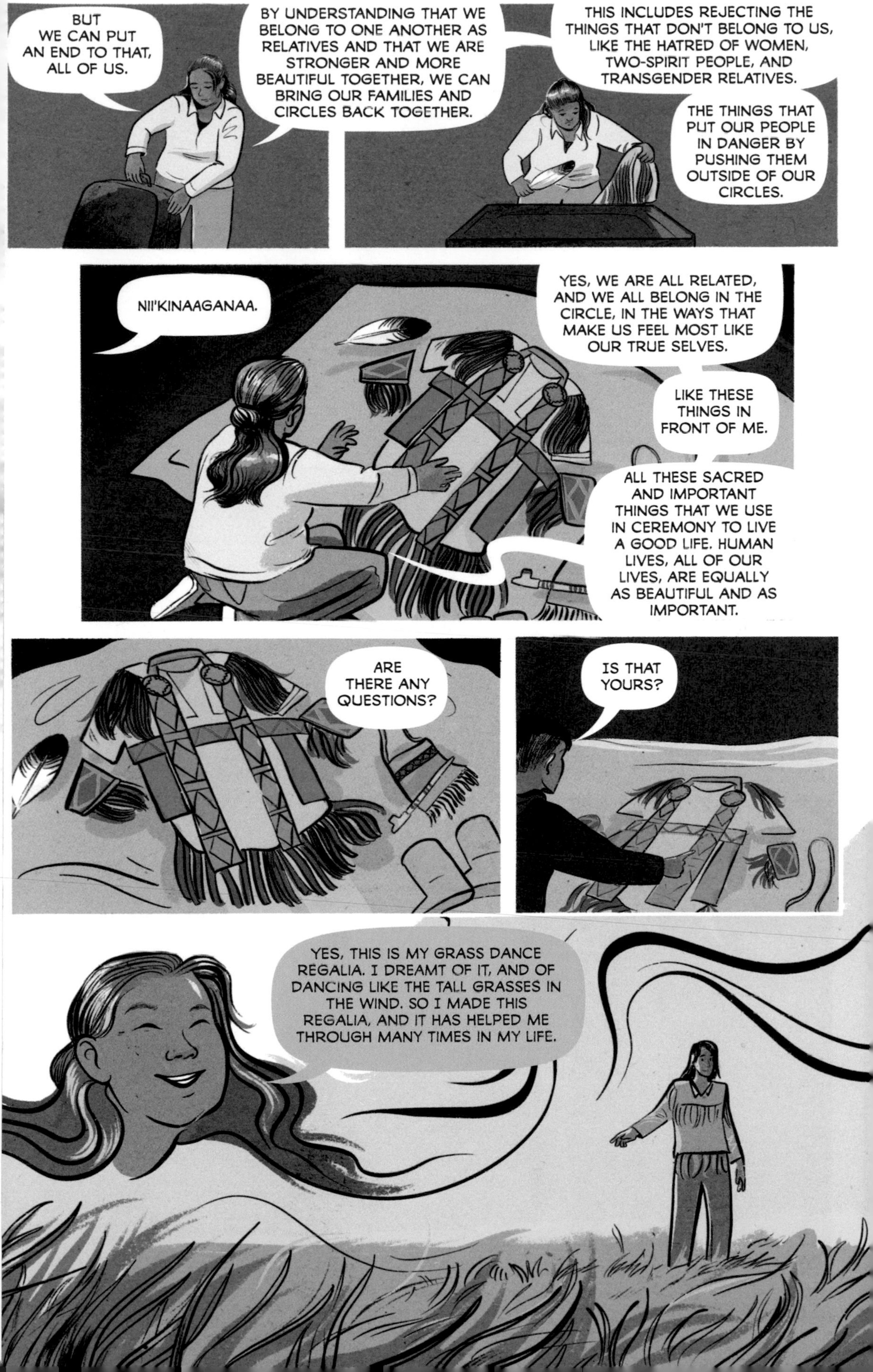
BUT WE CAN PUT AN END TO THAT, ALL OF US.
BY UNDERSTANDING THAT WE BELONG TO ONE ANOTHER AS RELATIVES AND THAT WE ARE STRONGER AND MORE BEAUTIFUL TOGETHER, WE CAN BRING OUR FAMILIES AND CIRCLES BACK TOGETHER.
THIS INCLUDES REJECTING THE THINGS THAT DON'T BELONG TO US, LIKE THE HATRED OF WOMEN, TWO-SPIRIT PEOPLE, AND TRANSGENDER RELATIVES.
THE THINGS THAT PUT OUR PEOPLE IN DANGER BY PUSHING THEM OUTSIDE OF OUR CIRCLES.
NII'KINAAGANAA.
YES, WE ARE ALL RELATED, AND WE ALL BELONG IN THE CIRCLE, IN THE WAYS THAT MAKE US FEEL MOST LIKE OUR TRUE SELVES.
LIKE THESE THINGS IN FRONT OF ME.
ALL THESE SACRED AND IMPORTANT THINGS THAT WE USE IN CEREMONY TO LIVE A GOOD LIFE. HUMAN LIVES, ALL OF OUR LIVES, ARE EQUALLY AS BEAUTIFUL AND AS IMPORTANT.
ARE THERE ANY QUESTIONS?
IS THAT YOURS?
YES, THIS IS MY GRASS DANCE REGALIA. I DREAMT OF IT, AND OF DANCING LIKE THE TALL GRASSES IN THE WIND. SO I MADE THIS REGALIA, AND IT HAS HELPED ME THROUGH MANY TIMES IN MY LIFE.

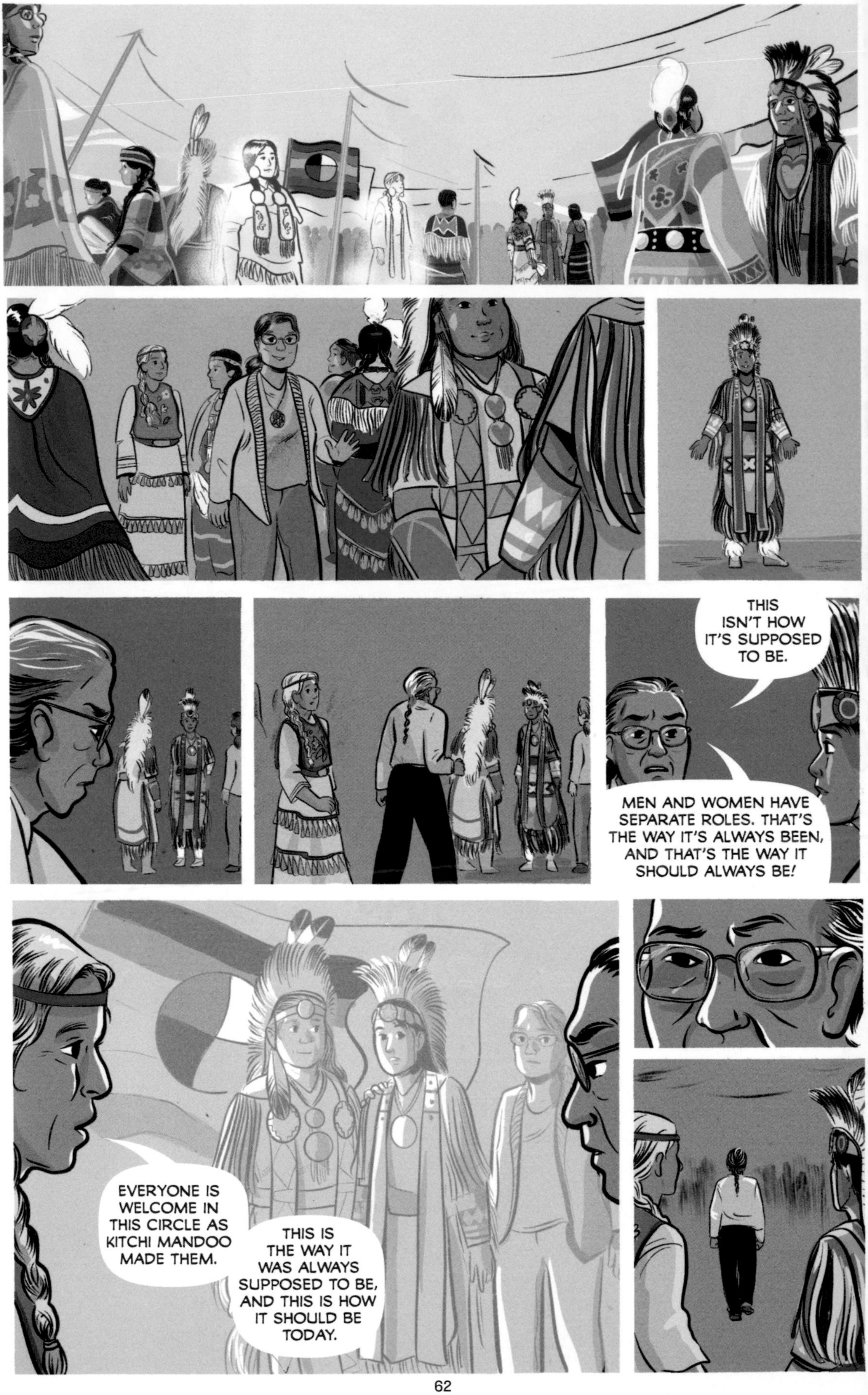
THIS ISN'T HOW IT'S SUPPOSED TO BE.
MEN AND WOMEN HAVE SEPARATE ROLES. THAT'S THE WAY IT'S ALWAYS BEEN, AND THAT'S THE WAY IT SHOULD ALWAYS BE!
EVERYONE IS WELCOME IN THIS CIRCLE AS KITCHI MANDOO MADE THEM.
THIS IS THE WAY IT WAS ALWAYS SUPPOSED TO BE, AND THIS IS HOW IT SHOULD BE TODAY.

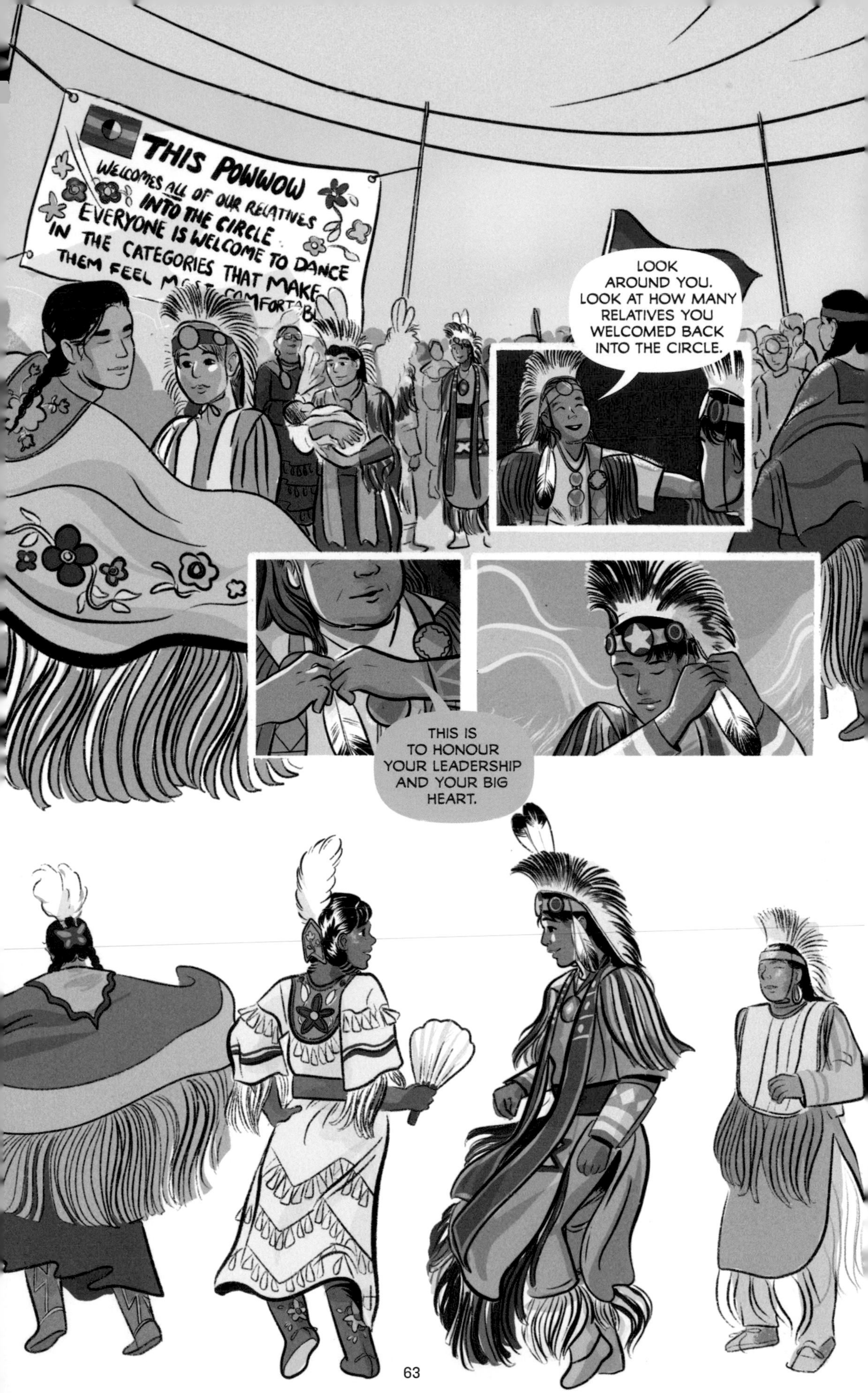
THIS POWWOW
WELCOMES ALL OF OUR RELATIVES
INTO THE CIRCLE
EVERYONE IS WELCOME TO DANCE
IN THE CATEGORIES THAT MAKE
THEM FEEL M
LOOK AROUND YOU. LOOK AT HOW MANY RELATIVES YOU WELCOMED BACK INTO THE CIRCLE.
THIS IS TO HONOUR YOUR LEADERSHIP AND YOUR BIG HEART.

What Does Two-Spirit Mean?

In Algonquian nations, humans are understood to possess the same beauty and mystery associated with other elements of the Natural World. Each child born into this world has a purpose and a destiny, and carries a divine gift. This belief is expressed in the Ojibwe term *aawi*, which literally means *he/she is who he/she is supposed to be*. Algonquian people who are gender fluid and/or sexually diverse (LGBTQI) are accepted as the part of the intentional design of the Spirit and Natural Worlds, and as such, it is a cultural taboo to critique or interfere with their identity, role, or life journey.

During the early colonial period, Canada and various church groups that ran Indian Residential and Day Schools disrupted this cultural imperative and introduced homophobic and transphobic attitudes across the nation. As Indigenous LGBTQI people recovered from generations of oppression and shaming, they began to gather and share their stories and experiences. At the third gathering of Native American Gays and Lesbians in Manitoba in 1990, Dr. Myra Laramee introduced the term *Two-Spirit people*, and it was quickly adopted by those in attendance.

Two-Spirit is an umbrella term that provides a window into the many Indigenous Nations and societies that honoured and respected their community members who were LGBTQI. There are over 150 words and terms in various Indigenous languages that describe this diversity. The name Two-Spirit reconnects Indigenous LGBTQI to the Spiritual and Natural Worlds.

Because of the shame that was introduced to our communities, many Two-Spirit youth experience teasing, bullying, shaming, and violence because people do not want to understand who they are or accept they have a respected place in their families and communities. This discrimination has increased the rate of suicide among Two-Spirit people and results in many Two-Spirit youth becoming homeless and living in poverty. However, as we begin to decolonize and reconcile from past harms, and as this story informs us, we must continue to provide the nurturance, love, and acceptance that Two-Spirit youth crave from their families and communities.

Albert McLeod
www.albertmcleod.com
April 1, 2020